CADE

The Five Shifter Rules

Always put your mate before yourself.

Respect another shifter's mate.

Do nothing to expose the existence of shifters.

Do no unnecessary harm to shifters or humans.

Respect all nonhumans.

V.A. Dold

Copyright 2014 by V.A. Dold

ISBN–13: 9780990523550
ISBN–10: 0990523551

Print edition March 2014

Cade: Le Beau Brothers

Table of Contents

V.A. Dold

This is Dedicated

To all of my readers and fans of the Le Beau
Series, I appreciate you more than I can say.

Thank you to my friends and family who cheered
me on and believed in me even more than I
believed in myself.

And thank you, Tina and Carolyn, the best editors
a girl could ask for.

...You all helped make this possible.

   ...Enjoy the adventure!

CADE

Le Beau Brothers
Book 1

By
V.A. Dold

Cade: Le Beau Brothers

V.A. Dold

Prologue– The Plan

"Emma, we need to take matters into our own hands or the boy's will never find their mates." Isaac Le Beau set his snifter down before he crushed the glass in frustration. "We have seven virile, grown sons, who, after two hundred years, still haven't found their mates. If we don't step in and give a hand to the wolf– Goddess, Luperca, our sons may spend their lives alone, without children to raise and without their other half to love. Dang it, I want some grandchildren while I'm still young enough to enjoy them."

He slowly raised his head and gazed at Emma, the love of his life. She was a unique blend of Romanian gypsy heritage and a very powerful voodoo priestess. Even after two centuries her exotic, sparkling dark eyes and compact, soft, killer curves left him breathless. Some would classify her as a big, beautiful woman. He just called her 'sex on a stick.' He swore she controlled every beat of his heart.

The warmth and agreement in those mesmerizing eyes silently prompted him to continue.

1

Cade: Le Beau Brothers

"Would you do your high–priestess voodoo thing and ask the spirits to identify their mates? With some influence, we could bring them together, so the boys can recognize them on their own," Isaac offered. "I don't want to force a meeting; simply provide the opportunity. How about it, will you give it a try?"

He knew Emma wouldn't deny him.

"Of course, I'll perform the ritual. But, I can't give you any guarantees. All I can do is try. If we are truly blessed, Luperca will appear to me and give this endeavor her approval. I want our sons happy, and I'd love to have a dozen grandchildren running around the house, too."

Isaac opened his arms wide, inviting Emma to slide onto his lap. He buried his face into her hair, breathing in her unique scent. The familiar fragrance calmed him like nothing else. He was confident everything would change for his sons very soon. Isaac could hardly wait for each of them to meet their one true mate. No wolf should go fourteen hundred years alone.

*****

Two weeks later, they were enjoying the cool breeze coming off the river as it drifted through the open windows. A secret little smile lit up Emma's entire face, and her fingers tapped a lively tune on her crystal wine glass. He knew that expression well.

"Out with it, Emma," Isaac said with a grin of his own. "What is it you're dying to tell me?" He waited patiently for her to tell him her grand news.

Emma actually bounced in her seat. "I received answers from the Goddess," she clapped her hands excitedly. "Cade's mate is in New Orleans right now. Her name is Anna James. The Goddess said she has had many unhappy years, but is now open to finding her one true love. Isn't that fantastic? Two days from now she is destined to be in Jackson Square, and then she will stop to eat lunch at Crescent City Brewhouse. She'll be in the bar around eleven–thirty. As for the rest of the boys, the Goddess said we must have patience. She'll grant me visions in my dreams or come to me for each of them when the time is right."

A surge of excited energy rushed through him as a hundred butterflies took up residence in his stomach.

This must be what it feels like to win the lottery, he thought.

"We'll have to move fast. We need to think of a way to get Cade there at the right time."

"Maybe we can come up with a way to use Jackson Square? Cade sits there so often it might be an option," Emma offered.

"Maybe."

He rubbed his chin, his forehead crinkled in deep thought. "First we need to get him out of his home office and into the French Quarter. The bank called yesterday about a restaurant up for sale. I'll have them schedule a meeting with Cade to review our investments and recommend this new opportunity." He tapped his chin as the plan took shape, mumbling as he worked it out. Isaac stood, paced across the room, prowling like the animal he was. He couldn't think properly sitting down.

Cade: Le Beau Brothers

As he strode back and forth, he noted Emma had settled into an easy chair to watch him.

"That'll get him to the city," he thought aloud as he continued to tap his finger on his chin. "You're right about his constant people–watching. I'm sure he'll take a walk and perhaps sit a while. That is a possibility…" Isaac cupped his jaw in his hand and rubbed the coarse stubble.

A satisfied smile tugged at his lips. "I've got it! I'll ask him to meet me for lunch at Crescent City at eleven–thirty. Richie tends the bar, and he'll know the mating signs. When Cade arrives, Goddess willing, he'll sense his mate. I'll have Richie tell him I won't be able to make it. If I'm not there for lunch, he will be free to spend time with her."

Smile broadening, he folded his arms across his chest and nodded. They had a solid plan. In less than a week, he could have his first daughter–in–law. Isaac settled into his leather captain's chair. "I'll arrange everything with Richie." He felt two hundred years younger, like the bold, robust young man who had swept his mate off her feet. By the wistful expression, Emma wore, he must look it, too.

As he sipped his rich, sweet cognac, he imagined a baby in Emma's lap, sleeping peacefully while a toddler played with blocks on the floor. His sigh brought her attention to him with a raised brow. She would laugh if she knew what he was dreaming.

A smile continued to pull at his lips. He couldn't help it. He was very pleased with his little romance ambush. Positive it would be successful. Cade was in for a wonderful surprise in two days' time.

"Now that we have the plan, what do you think she will be like? Did the Goddess give you any hints?"

She laughed. "No, you silly man. The Goddess doesn't have time for things like that."

"You know, he has always favored curvy women. I sure hope she isn't skinny. He might not even look at her if she is." A little shiver ran through him. "The last woman he dated looked a lot like you. Remember that? She was a plus sized beauty. Cade never said anything, but Marcus drove him crazy with that 'Oedipus' nickname," he laughed as he recalled the antics of the boys.

"You're right; he does like a woman with meat on her bones. All the boys do."

Chapter 1

Five Years Earlier

Anna James took a seat facing the private investigator, Todd. It was a dreary Monday morning; even the weather seemed ominous as she waited for the bomb to drop. An hour earlier, Todd had called and requested she meet with him at the corner diner. Anna couldn't believe what she saw. He had handed her a manila envelope bursting with evidence. Turning it over, she wondered how the seams possibly held the volume.

She stared at it for a moment, her hands shaking harder than a craps gambler on a losing streak. As she lifted the first photo from the bundle, the breath was sucked out of her lungs. She would not be sick. He had cheated on her. Again.

Her marriage's decline was so gradual. She'd missed all the signs. Like a creeping line of mold that became a steady decay of both the physical and emotional aspects of their relationship.

She had to admit to herself, her love for Tim had died a slow death. Based on the evidence she held, he felt the same.

Letting out a long shaky breath, she had a decision to make. Her gut reaction was to walk out the door and never look back.

I need to call Rose. She'll help me decide what to do.

Rose was her best friend, her rock. Her voice of reason.

Returning from her meeting with Todd, she sat on her couch and considered her options. If not for her two young sons, she would leave right then. But she couldn't bring herself to be that selfish, to deny Thomas and John their father. So, she'd stay and take her marriage for what it was, a necessary evil. She would pursue a new life once the children were grown and out of the house. At least that way, the boys would grow up in a two–parent home.

After a long conversation with Rose, she had made a difficult decision. Standing to call it a night, she ended her call to Rose. She had a plan. A long–term plan. Yawning, she stumbled to her cold, empty bed. Soon she found herself in a dream world she had never experienced. The colors were brilliant, and she felt everything she touched as if she were awake.

She stretched on the slick, crimson sheets. The texture was very sleek and slippery. A royal blue silk nightgown wrapped her body. She was running her hands down her body, admiring the gown, when warm hands drew her against a hard chest. Those amazing arms held her gently, all through the night.

A beam of bright sunshine across her pillow was her 'good morning' welcome. She was alone in the bed as usual. She smiled as she recalled her delicious dream.

Cade: Le Beau Brothers

All the romance novels I've read must have manifested in my dreams. I can live with that, she grinned.

The dreams continued to visit her night after night, slowly taking on more detail. First she saw the dark, multicolored hair with its luxurious shine and velvety waves. Then she was able to make out his stunning, hazel green eyes. Sometime later his full, kissable lips came into focus. From head to toe, he gradually took a complete and solid form. Close to two years of unhurried, delectable development. What a hot, sexy man he'd become.

At some point, they began to carry on conversations about everything. In one dream, they had discussed hair and eye color and how it often reflected traits of different nationalities.

"Cher, what part of the world is lucky enough to claim a gorgeous redhead with 'melt me' hazel eyes as an ancestor?" he asked.

Anna rolled her eyes, and she smiled. He was so over the top sometimes. "I'm mostly German, with a little bit of everything mixed in," she said. "What are you?" She pulled from his arms to look at him. "No, let me guess."

She raked her fingers through his hair, drawing a deep moan from him. "Your dark hair and eyes and straight nose say you're from Europe. And the rest of you," her eyes trailed to his bared chest and abs, "is one hundred percent from my mind."

He laughed. "You are close, mon amour. I am Romanian and Cajun. My mother says I am a perfect blend of her gypsy features and my father's Cajun heritage."

Anna agreed. That was a perfect description.

One of her favorite dreams was the first time he'd kissed her.

She was at a dance in a beautiful Victorian home. The gardens off the terraces were in bloom, adding a heady floral perfume to the air. She couldn't put her finger on the scent exactly. There were layers, roses, carnations, lilies, damp earth and something else that eluded her. Benches circled a three–tiered fountain, the cascade of water made a music all its own.

The ballroom's double doors that led to the terrace were flung wide open. White lace curtains ruffled in the breeze. Music from an eight–piece band played in the far corner of the room. A huge expanse of gleaming hardwood waited as her dance floor.

As she glanced around the ballroom, her fantasy man entered through the main doors across the way. He stopped and slowly scanned the room as if searching for someone. His eyes locked onto hers as he prowled the length, determined to reach her. Without a word, he took her into his arms and guided her in a romantic waltz that swept the room. Commanding and sure of himself, he never once took his gaze from her, nor did he miss a step.

When the music died, he dipped her slowly, romantically. As he raised her, he pulled her to him. With utter confidence, he kissed her. She had been dying to kiss him for ages. He enticed her to open to him, he slipped in and plundered her mouth. Exploring every curve and hollow, their tongues danced to a tune all their own.

Cade: Le Beau Brothers

The heat and hunger burned intensely; it was exhilarating. The kiss seemed to go on forever before he released her lips. Breathing heavily, he continued to hold her as he leaned his forehead against hers. He seemed to be fighting to regain his composure. She was a bit disappointed. She hadn't wanted the kiss to end. He was a sweet, delicious slice of heaven that took her breath away.

"You never told me your name," Anna began.

An instant later, the dream ended before she learned his name or saw where the dance would lead. She'd laid in bed, awake, a hot and achy mess with little relief.

She knew almost everything about her fantasy man. He was born on the sixteenth day of June. He was the oldest in his family, the first born of seven children, all boys. They were extremely close, best friends even. He one time joked that when they were combined, they were a force to be reckoned with. She wasn't quite sure what he meant by that.

The one thing she didn't know was his name. Every time she asked, the dream abruptly stopped before he could answer. The same happened if he asked her. The situation was frustrating as hell. As if someone or something prevented him from giving this information. Eventually, she stopped asking. This was the only place she could be with him, and she hated when the dream was taken from her. To make the best of the situation, they made up pet names for each other. He called her cher, which Cajuns use as an endearment. She called him Babe or Baby.

V.A. Dold

*****

She'd dreamed of her man for three years when her next favorite dream took place.

She was in a lovely little cottage, very airy and bright. As she toured her dream house, she noted the decorations were exactly how she would picture her perfect home. If she lived there–she lived alone. There were no indications of a man to be found.

Lounging on the front porch swing, enjoying the cool breeze, she watched in fascination as a fancy, red sports car pulled up. The driver's door swung open, and Babe eased his long, muscular body out. Their eyes locked, and he devoured her with his gaze. Even from twenty feet away, he made her temperature rise.

In a heartbeat, he was across the driveway and up her steps. As he extended his hand to her, his eyes smoldered with a hunger that excited her. "I want to make love to you," he whispered.

She had waited for this moment for so long, all she could do was nod and follow him as he led her to the bedroom.

He gently sat her on the edge of the mattress before he proceeded to light a dozen candles scattered around the room. Funny, she hadn't noticed them before, but this was a dream, so she went with it.

After the last candle blazed, he turned to her and started to unbutton his shirt, one excruciating button at a time. By the time he reached her, his shirt hung open allowing her eyes to feast on his chiseled chest and abs. He was absolutely gorgeous, simply looking at him made her mouth water and her pulse race.

11

Cade: Le Beau Brothers

Helping her to her feet, he slowly unbuttoned her blouse. Brushing the silky material off her shoulders, it floated to the floor. She swore she saw flames of desire in his eyes as he drank her in. He grasped her hands gently and placed them on his chest as if giving her permission to explore at her leisure.

She ran her palms up and eased his shirt off his shoulders. As the material slid down his arms, her fingertips followed, tracing every line and curve of his muscular arms. When she moved her hands to his waist, he reached around and unclasped her bra, eased the straps down her arms and released her aching breasts. His breath hitched at the first sight of her bare skin from the waist up.

Her estranged husband had repeatedly told her she was fat; he couldn't stand to look at her. She was too self–conscious to stand naked in front of anyone, she even avoided mirrors. In front of her perfect man, her self–consciousness increased exponentially. No denying it, she was plus sized with a bit more to love. A size sixteen with extra padding and rolls where rolls shouldn't be, and God forbid, cellulite. She hated to look at her own body.

When she moved to cover herself out of embarrassment, he took her hands and placed them at her sides. Gazing deeply into her eyes, he said, "Please don't hide yourself from me. To me, you are the most beautiful woman in the world. I want to appreciate you for a moment."

She stood stiffly, holding her breath, waiting for him to see all of her extra curves and rolls. He had to see her stretch marks from bearing her children. At any moment, he would run from the room. But he didn't. Instead, his eyes blazed with heat. How could he look at her with such desire?

His gaze returned to her face. Maintaining eye contact, he loosened his belt and popped the button on his jeans. "Should I remove them, or would you prefer to do it?" His sexy, lopsided grin melted her shyness.

But, her hands shook so badly, she was sure she would never get her fingers to cooperate. "I think you should," Anna whispered.

He hooked his thumbs into the waist of his jeans, pushed down his pants and boxers as one. His rock hard erection bobbed brazenly as if begging for her attention. She saw a drop of moisture already escaping. Stepping out of his jeans, he reached for her waistband. "May I?" he asked hopefully.

She cleared her throat but didn't trust her voice to work right. In the end, all she dared do was nod again.

With smoldering hunger in his eyes, he slid her jeans to her ankles. He followed their descent until he was kneeling before her. Freeing her feet, he wrapped his fingers around her ankles before he skimmed them up her legs to her hips. His fingers slipped into the waistband of her panties, and they followed the path of her jeans.

He leaned forward, and, with gentle pressure, encouraged her to widen her stance. When he took her into his mouth, she gasped. It had been so long. Her legs almost buckled with his first lick. He had to help her remain standing as he lapped and suckled to his heart's content. When she reached the edge of her orgasm, he pulled away and stood. His lips and chin glistened with the evidence of her arousal.

Cade: Le Beau Brothers

Easing her down, he joined her on the bed. Babe spent the rest of the night making wild, passionate love to her. Twice.

Still unsure of herself after years with a man who berated her, she hadn't had the courage to take him in her hand and caress him.

Maybe next time, she thought.

Shock spread through her when she woke the next morning, sore in places that hadn't been used in years. How was that possible?

Babe came to her every night at her little cottage. Some nights they would sit on the swing and talk for hours, other nights they would explore each other until dawn. She had gotten to know so much about him.

After a year like this with him, Anna had her third favorite dream.

She noticed as he joined her on the swing; he was very quiet. He had something to say but was apprehensive to say it.

Finally, he took a deep breath. "Cher, I have something I need to tell you about myself. This may scare you, but I feel guilty not telling you what I truly am."

She reached out and took his hand in hers. "Don't worry, you can tell me. It's okay."

Afraid to look into her eyes and see rejection, he examined the floor instead. "I'm a shifter. I can change into a wolf." He stiffened, as he waited for her response. He appeared to expect the worst. After what felt like an hour but was only a minute, he glanced up.

She was smiling at him, waiting for him to look at her. "Are you really? I wanted you to be a shifter when I made you up, and honestly, I was kind of

14

disappointed when I thought you were only human."

Tilting his head, he wore a look of disbelief. "You're kidding, right? You're actually happy about this?"

"Well, yeah! I wanted you to be a shifter. I'm ecstatic. Can I see you shift?"

Still looking a bit wary of her reaction, he slowly stood and took a few steps away. "Are you sure you want me to do this?"

"Of course. Can you change without a full moon?"

"Shifters can change anytime they want. We're not the mythical werewolves. I'll count to three and shift. Are you ready?

Anna nodded.

"One, two, three." Instantly a beautiful, huge, black and silver wolf stood on her porch.

Anna gasped and squealed with excitement, so thrilled she didn't know what to do. She wanted to pet him but didn't know if she was allowed.

As if sensing her indecision, he approached her and laid his head on her lap.

She sank her fingers into his fur. The texture was incredibly soft. He turned his head this way and that, trying to get her to scratch in just the right places. After several minutes, he stepped away and in a heartbeat her fully clothed man was on her porch again.

"Did you like my wolf, cher?" he asked with a grin as if knowing she had.

"You know I did, so quit fishing for compliments." She giggled.

He let out a loud laugh, scooped her in his arms and carried her to bed for the rest of the night.

Both of them were so happy together in their dreams. Her only regret was the dream world wasn't real.

Chapter 2

Six Months Earlier

Anna wiped her brow with a leftover napkin from her fast food lunch. The drive from Denver to New Orleans in her rented moving van had been long. She smiled as she sat a little straighter in the driver's seat, proud that she had managed it by herself in just two days. The adrenaline–laced excitement over her first adventure as a single woman had fueled her the entire way. Living here had always been a dream. The minute Thomas and John graduated from college; she followed that dream.

According to her watch, she had an hour until she met with a realtor to tour apartments. She set the alarm on her smartphone and closed her eyes.

An hour later she walked through gate number eleven with the realtor. She felt like an old gym sock. Then, like a dog when someone knocks on the door, all her senses perked up as she stepped into a lush, plant–filled courtyard. Instantly she was transported to her own little oasis. Ten minutes later she'd paid the deposit and first month's rent for a small two–bedroom apartment right outside the French Quarter.

Cade: Le Beau Brothers

To celebrate her first night in her new place, she took a glass of wine to the courtyard. This was her first chance to sit at the little-wrought iron table close to the lion's head fountain. The sound as the water splashed and gurgled relaxed her as she rubbed the ache from her sore muscles. Everything about the fountain reminded her of the one in her dreams. They looked different, but the moment she closed her eyes she was back at the Victorian home on the terrace.

*****

The next morning she paused in front of the bathroom mirror.

Do I look any different? Will people be able to tell I'm single? She laughed at herself; what a crazy notion.

As she searched for gray hairs, all she saw in the mirror was the same old, average Anna. She had great hair, the perfect color of auburn. Rose called it fox red.

My eyes are nice, she thought as she leaned closer to her reflection, although there were a few more laugh lines than before.

They were hazel, a mostly green version of hazel. She smiled at the color. Today they were a bright, vibrant green that reflected her excitement.

The rest of the reflection was no surprise; she saw a basic mid–forties woman. Turning sideways, she sucked in her belly.

Oh, well, I have to work with what I have.

What she couldn't see in the mirror was the unswerving confidence that attracted people to her wherever she went.

V.A. Dold

*****

After three months, Anna's apartment had begun to take shape. Her walls were still pretty bare, but she was particular about what she wanted and willing to wait to find it.

She stepped back from the bedroom wall she had just painted a lovely shade of warm cinnamon. When she purchased the paint, she had wondered if it was too bold for the room, but it looked great.

Suddenly her phone chimed the arrival of a new email. Glancing at the sender name, she cringed. It was Tim, her ex. Ever since she moved from Denver, he had been constantly emailing. Thankfully he didn't know her phone number. What could he possibly want now?

Oh. Hell, no!!!!

The email was his way of announcing he had moved.

To New Orleans!

What was he playing at, following her here?

Tim wanted to meet her for coffee. The sucker she used to be was gone. She couldn't be rude to people, not even jackasses. She decided she would speak to him once and be done with him.

Anna took a seat across from him in the booth.

What the heck did he move here for, and what does he want?

"Hello, sweetheart. I've missed you."

She struggled not to laugh in his face. "What do you want, Tim?"

"I wanted to see you," he pouted.

"Sure you did," she scoffed. "Now tell me what you really want."

He frowned at her. "I'm broke. Between the move and other expenses, I need a loan. Can you lend me some money until I find a job?"

She stood without a word and walked out of the café. As she walked to her place, she shook her head at his ludicrous behavior.

Apparently he doesn't want me, and yet, can't live without me. Whatever.

Present Day

Stretching, she padded into the kitchen for her morning cup of coffee. She poured a cup as she waited for her laptop to power up. Today she was finishing some online promotions for a Fortune 100 client, and she needed all her cylinders firing.

By 10 a.m., she was done for the day and strolled through the Quarter. Morning was her favorite time. The streets and sidewalks were freshly washed. And, the sounds of deliverymen hauling boxed produce filled the air. Tourists with cups of café au lait passed by, reminding her to stop for a cup. The activity felt like the heartbeat of the city.

She was looking for artwork to hang in her new home, and Jackson Square was just the place to start her search. There was nothing like discovering the perfect piece among the local artists.

Maybe today I will find the perfect painting.

She hummed to herself quietly as she walked around the Square. Nothing appealed to her again today.

Sighing, she headed to Crescent City Brewhouse for a glass of beer and burger. Richie would cheer her up. She had met him when she sat at his bar for the first time twelve years prior, and he had taken her order. She often returned to visit with him ever since. They had become good friends, and he was one of the few friends she had in the Quarter.

Walking through the restaurant door was like coming home for her. She loved the walls– stucco with ragged patches of the old brick showing through.

I wish my apartment had these walls.

She ran her hand along the Grand thirty–six–foot golden oak bar with its classic brass foot rail. Most of the tall bar chairs were vacant–the lunch crowd hadn't started yet.

Perched on a bar chair, she checked her phone for messages while she waited for Richie.

Scowling, she stared at the email that had popped up on her screen. No way! Not again.

She read it one more time. The rotten piece of dog excrement actually asked to meet with her again for about the hundredth time.

Anna,
I need to see you. Meet me at the diner ASAP.
Tim

"You have got to be kidding me," she snarled. Her ex-husband was after money again. She'd been through this email routine enough times to know it always came down to money and his lack of it. "Stupid S–O–B," she growled at her offending cell phone.

Richie looked at her, surprised.

"Sorry, Richie, but this," she waved the phone around again, "this requires strong language, or maybe a Mac truck to run him over with, repeatedly. Tim is after money again. What kind of lowlife keeps harassing his ex for money because he can't hold a job?"

Now Richie looked appalled. "He's at it again? Darling, I'm so sorry. I don't understand him at all." He leaned across the bar. "Are you going to be all right?"

"Yes, I'll be fine," she sighed.

The man was an idiot.

The problem was, he couldn't get the idea through his head they were done.

She heard footsteps behind her and glanced up as a handsome man walked past with a pretty woman on his arm. The sight reminded her she hadn't had a date yet as a single woman.

"Hey, Richie, you got any cute single friends? I haven't been in the dating world in a long time."

Richie chuckled. "I'll check around for you. I'm sure I'll think of someone."

Not wanting to think about the ex–rat bastard anymore, she decided a visit with her baby was in order. At least until she found her real–life fantasy man. Lord knows she'd earned one. He was always a perfect distraction. Thinking of him made her sigh and feel a little better.

He was tall, like six–foot–three inches of tall. Better yet, he was built like a brick house with wide shoulders, pecks to lick and nibble, and his six–pack abs made her squirm in her seat just thinking about them. That body was designed for sex, plain and simple. Add to that, a face that was cover–model handsome– not pretty–boy cover model, but the rugged ones. Oh, but his eyes, a stunning green hazel, which became bright glowing green when he shifted to his wolf form. God, she loved that hot sexy shifter.

Why can't he be real? I mean really, it could happen, right? She thought to herself.

Anna stared blindly at the wall. As the fantasy began, her baby greeted her.

Cher, I've missed you. He reached out and caressed her cheek as he gazed into her eyes. She felt him tunneling his fingers into her hair. Carefully he cupped the back of her head as he slowly brought his lips to hers. He savored her, gently sliding his tongue along the seam of her lips to encourage her to open to him…

Right then, Richie plunked down the beer she'd ordered, very effectively ending the daydream right when the kiss was about to get good. She wanted to smack him.

Cade Le Beau had finished with his personal banker and financial advisor. A new restaurant was in his future, a very profitable one, based on the financials. Checking the time, he had forty–five minutes to waste before he had lunch with his father.

He knew the French Quarter so well he didn't even pay attention as he walked. He lifted the hair off his neck to allow the soft breeze to cool his skin. Cade preferred to use the sunny side of the street with fewer pedestrians.

As he dodged a tourist studying a map, a vision of the woman from his dreams popped into his brain. The one from Jackson Square he had desperately wanted to meet the year before.

Cher, I've missed you. He reached out and caressed her cheek as he gazed into her beautiful eyes. They were a stormy brown today. For a moment, he wondered what had upset her. He had to taste those soft lips. So he tunneled his fingers into her hair and cupped the back of her head as he slowly brought his lips to hers. Savoring her lips, he gently slid his tongue along the seam to encourage her to open to him...

What the hell! Where'd she go? His wolf growled.

As the vision abruptly ended, Cade stumbled to a stop outside the open doorway of Crescent City Brewhouse. From the sidewalk, passersby could peer into the restaurant with a clear view of the long, solid wood bar lined with people on bar chairs waiting for their lunches.

The restaurant wasn't what caused him to hesitate. Once he regained his balance, he felt a force pulling him, drawing him inside. Unable to stop, he followed his wolf's instincts and went in. Completely shocked, he stopped in his tracks.

It was the woman he'd just been fantasizing about.

Sitting at the bar.

Alone.

Her long auburn hair flowed down her back in lustrous, thick waves. Her blue jeans and a tight white T–shirt hugged all her curves perfectly. Best of all, there was the most delicious aroma coming from her. The scent was like warm toast and honey. He tried to will her to turn around so he could see her eyes. In his dreams, her eyes were amazing pools of hazel green. They showed her every expression and mood. If she was angry they turned dark and more brown, but if she was excited or happy they were an intense green. They literally were the windows to her soul.

He'd only seen her the one time, and then only from the side. He hadn't actually seen her face. He had been rushing to a meeting he was late for. She'd been shopping the local artists and had a short, pudgy man with her at the time. He'd almost blown off his meeting in order to introduce himself and ask her to join him for a drink or dinner. But as he wrestled with indecision, his phone rang. His brother, Stefan, had been wondering where he was. As he answered the call, she'd turned and strolled down the street and out of his life.

After he fell to sleep that night, his fantasy woman, Cher, appeared. She was the same woman as the one from the square. Cade hadn't realized she was a real woman until that moment. Stunned, he felt bereft. He'd missed his opportunity to meet her in real life. For the better part of a week, after he'd lost her, he'd walked around the Quarter with the hope of spotting her again. He'd spent weeks kicking himself for not walking up to her immediately. Answering Stefan's call had cost him more than he had known.

He'd been desperate to find her in an unnaturally intense way. When he hadn't seen her again and had no way of contacting her, he'd given up, even though, every fiber of his being screamed for him to find her. She'd been the utmost gorgeous woman he'd ever laid eyes on. Worse yet, his need was compounded by the fact that she was the only woman that both he and his wolf wanted. He had desperately wanted to ask her where she lived or get her phone number, but he was terrified she'd stop coming to his dreams if he did. Every time he had tried to learn her name, the dreams ended. If he asked for something as important as her address, there was no telling what would happen. Better to take what he could get in these dreams than lose her completely. Even though he hadn't actually met her, he had felt he was having a love affair with her.

His wolf instincts rose to the surface. Like a puppet on a string, he was drawn to her. As he got within five feet of her, he realized she was upset. Who or what had upset her? The wolf and the man wanted to tear and rend the offender. He searched the room, trying to locate what or who needed killing for this unforgivable offense. As he listened to her angry words, he realized it had been some kind of message that had upset her. An email.

*****

Anna paused her angry tirade as she felt the presence of someone behind her. She sensed a major shift in energy, which made the hair on the back of her neck stand on end. Slowly she turned, and her breath caught in her throat.

A gorgeous stranger stood not more than five feet from her with his powerfully built arms crossed. He stared at her in a strange way that made her shiver in the May heat. She'd swear he was ready to pounce at any moment. His head was lowered to peer down at her. She practically swooned, as she looked him up and down from his long muscular calves and thighs encased in tight denim to his taut stomach and wide shoulders.

She was openly, unabashedly staring at him.

He had a breathtakingly handsome face, with a strong jawline and high cheekbones. His face was freshly shaven and so smooth she wanted to caress his cheek.

My God, his blue jeans and T–shirt hugged his chest and hips with a precision that was almost sinful.

I know I'm thinking in circles, but I mean look at him, she thought. *I want to stroke him like a cat.*

Repeatedly.

And as often as possible.

She was mesmerized like a deer caught in headlights. Even though he hid them behind sunglasses, she was sure he had heart–stopping eyes. His grin alone could knock a woman's socks off.

Suddenly, her stare turned into a shocked expression.

It's him! This is the man I made up in my mind. The perfect man of my dreams. The one that I've been dreaming about for years, with that amazing six–pack of abs. How could this be possible? I made him up– there's no way he's real. Oh, shit! We'd done 'things' in those dreams, and I had just been kissing him in my fantasy!

Holy Hannah! He's completely sinful from top to bottom.

He heard her say 'Holy Hannah' in his head. A wolf shifter is only able to hear the voice of one person telepathically. *MATE!* This glorious, sexy, curvy woman was his one true mate, the other half of his soul. No wonder he'd been so frantic to find her a year ago. The instant attraction that had pulled at him had been the call of one mate to the other.

He grinned, his eyes twinkling with amusement hidden behind his dark sunglasses. He almost felt guilty eavesdropping on her thoughts but dang she thought loudly.

Hold on–she thought she was just kissing me in her fantasy? Is it possible we are sharing these dreams?

"Hello," she smiled at him nervously.

He closed his eyes as her voice hit him like a rogue wave at sea. The sensation knocked the breath right out of him. For his kind, there was only one true mate for each male. The male recognized his mate by a special scent designed specifically for him. The essence would draw him so strongly he wouldn't be able to deny its pull. And when he heard his mate's voice, the effect would be like the world opened for him. His animal soul would recognize its other half, and there would be no doubt.

And right now his animal soul rejoiced and hopped around like an excited puppy. Lastly, he would be able to communicate with her telepathically. Check, check, and check.

She was his mate. With one simple word, she had reached deep into his animal soul, enchanted his animal half and changed his life forever.

Just gazing at her made his whole body sizzle. He was instantly flooded with desire. Not to mention hard enough to pound nails. But, she was apprehensive, he could smell it.

V.A. Dold

"Hello," he said softly as he removed his sunglasses. He was trying to make her feel more comfortable around him. It didn't work. Actually, it made her heart race even faster. He heard it thumping wildly in her chest.

She was astounded. His voice was deep, almost enthralling and flowed over her like a soft caress. The rumbling tambour made her instantly hot. And those hazel–green eyes, even more amazing than she had imagined. She didn't think he could be any hotter. Boy, was she wrong. His intense, hungry stare made her stomach fill with butterflies, and her temperature rose about a thousand degrees. She had never seen a man this handsome. At least not in real life, men like him only lived in fantasies. Hers apparently.

Finally, she got a hold of herself. "Hi," she said again.

Geez, did I really say hello a second time? He must think I'm a complete moron. You have a vocabulary, Anna, you idiot. Use your words. You really need to work on this if you're going to start dating again.

He coughed, and it sounded like one of those fake coughs when you're trying to hide a laugh.

His gaze left her and went to the bar chair next to her. "Is this seat taken?"

"No, not at all." She was sure she would die from complete embarrassment. The moment he was next to her, his scent surrounded her. It made her heart pound harder.

Wow, he smells amazing, like warm chocolate and fresh baked bread.

Richie came over and smiled at him. He'd seen the whole thing play out.

"Well, hello, Mr. Le Beau, it's nice to see you again. By the way, your father called ten minutes ago. He was called into a meeting and has to cancel your lunch."

"Hello, Richie. I guess that leaves me without a lunch date." He was more than happy to hear his father had other plans. This made spending time with his mate so much easier.

He turned to her. "If I may ask, which beer are you drinking?"

Cade had worked hard to tone down his bayou boy accent for the business world, but this woman wiped all that hard work away. His lazy Cajun drawl was back with a vengeance.

She glanced at her glass and then back at him. "I'm having the Pilsner. What kind of beer do you normally like?

He nodded his head in approval. "I generally enjoy Pilsners as well. Dark beers don't hold much appeal for me."

He glanced at Richie. "The Pilsner, please."

He was hardly able to keep the silly grin off his face. He was sitting with the woman he had fantasized about for years having a beer! Everything about the situation seemed so easy. So normal.

He turned to her and extended his hand. "Allow me to introduce myself. I'm Cade Le Beau."

She reached out and blushed a little as she took his hand. "I'm Anna. Anna James."

Holding her gaze, he raised her hand to his lips and placed a gentle kiss on the back. "It's a pleasure to meet such a lovely lady." He had to stop himself from leaning forward. His wolf wanted to nuzzle her neck and inhale her scent. He wondered what her lips would feel like in real life. He fondly recalled the pleasure of making her lips swollen from his kisses and having her scream his name in ecstasy. He had wonderful memories of making love to her. And of exploring her luscious curves. Would she be like in his dreams? His wolf growled imagining her lush, soft body pressed against his just like in his visions.

She was mesmerized by the gallant kiss to her hand. It made her grin like a schoolgirl and heat exploded across her face.

Now, this is the perfect man. Wow, Finding a prince charming in this town sure didn't take long, she giggled to herself. *Who'd have thought perfect men fall into your lap in NOLA?*

He released her hand reluctantly. "Have you eaten lunch? I'm starving, and I'd love to have you join me."

Please say yes…

Startled, she stared at him wide–eyed.

Wait a minute, did I just hear him in my head, or had he said the last part out loud?

She wasn't sure because she'd been staring at the hand he'd kissed. She hesitated for a moment searching his face for a clue. "I would love to have lunch with you."

When Richie returned with his beer, Cade turned to him. "I'd like to enjoy the wonderful weather we're having with this beautiful woman. May we please have a table on the second-floor deck? I see the area is closed, but I'd take it as a personal favor if you would make this happen for me."

Cade: Le Beau Brothers

*****

"For you, Mr. Le Beau, anything." As she watched the exchange with Richie, the manager walked over and greeted Cade, shaking his hand like an old friend.

Now her curiosity was piqued. Who was this guy and how did he get all this special service? She was going to ask him once they were seated. The manager waved the hostess over and instructed her to take them upstairs to the balcony and send a waiter to them immediately.

Chapter 3

Lunch With Anna

On the upper level, she scanned the area as she took her seat. The air was filled with the riverboats playing music to attract tourists for a ride. Squinting in that direction, she tried to see the ship, but a building blocked her view. The sound of pedestrians drew her attention to the sidewalk below. People were walking to and from Jackson Square enjoying the beautiful weather.

Once they were alone, she peered at Cade. "If you don't mind my asking, who are you and how do you get such great service?"

He grinned a slow, slightly lopsided grin. "I'm part owner of this restaurant. I actually own bits and pieces all over the French Quarter, but this is one of my favorites."

Ho…ly….Cow!!!

Smoking hot and loaded!!!

She suddenly felt very inadequate.

What the heck is this guy doing having lunch with me? He looks to be about thirty years old, and I'm forty–five, not to mention a solid size sixteen. Granted,

Cade: Le Beau Brothers

I look closer to thirty–five, but still... Is he some kind of cougar chaser?

Hearing her concern, he realized he needed to fix this fast before she decided to get up and leave. As he searched for something to say…

She cleared her throat. "I'm going to be blunt here. You're a very handsome young man and obviously wealthy. Why is someone like you asking me to lunch instead of some gorgeous runway model?"

He resisted the need to reach out and take her hand into his. It took all his strength to hold back his wolf and take this slow. He wouldn't take the chance of losing her again.

He gazed into her eyes. "I'm told I look younger than I am. It must be really good genes. As for who I choose to have lunch with, I don't want some bony model with fluff for brains. I want you. A beautiful woman with a woman's body and a sharp mind." As he said the last part, his voice became low and held a hint of a growl.

Wanting to learn all about his mate, it was time to ask some questions. If, by chance, he lost her again, he wanted to know as much about her as possible so he could track her down. "So, Anna, do you live here in New Orleans or are you here on vacation?"

"I moved here about six months ago." She wasn't sure how much more to add.

"Do you live here alone, or do you have a family?" He wanted to know upfront who he may have to fight to claim his mate. Last time he'd seen her, she was with that man. He'd better be out of the picture. Just the thought of Anna with another male made him growl. His wolf practically went feral at the thought.

Anna's eyes rounded as predatory growls rolled from Cade.

Is he insane? Maybe I should make a run for the stairs?

When no visible threat came from him, she decided maybe it was nothing after all–she must have been hearing things. Maybe a dog had walked by and it had growled?

Well, time to air out the dirty laundry. Unable to look this gorgeous man in the face as she confessed the failure of her marriage, she wrung her hands in her lap.

"Actually, I'm single now. So, no, I live alone."

"Single now?"

"To tell the truth, my divorce was final about six months ago. I moved here for a fresh start. The problem is, my ex – followed me. Right before you walked up, I received an email from him. He wanted money, as usual."

His eyes narrowed dangerously. "That man is an idiot and a bastard."

Feeling like she needed to change the subject, she added, "I also have two grown sons who still live in Denver. Thomas turned twenty–four in May. I'm so proud of him. He majored in law enforcement and worked at the local sheriff's office all four years of school. When he graduated, he decided he didn't want to be a policeman. Maybe it was all the Sherlock Holmes he watched as a kid, but he struck out and opened his own private investigator service. He's doing really well, too."

"He sounds like someone I would really like to meet. You said you had two sons?"

Cade: Le Beau Brothers

"Yes. My youngest is John. He turned twenty–one in March, and as soon as he graduated college with his business degree, he joined Thomas at his PI agency. They're young, single, running their own business and have the world by the tail."

Right, then the waitress came to the table. "What may I get for you today, Mr. Le Beau?"

He gazed at her and smiled gently. "Would you like to share a couple of my favorites?"

She glanced up from her menu, and a smile lit her face. "That would be wonderful."

"Please bring us the crawfish étouffée and crabmeat stuffed shrimp."

The waitress hustled away to take care of their order, leaving them alone again.

His voice grew gentle. "I'm sorry to hear about what happened to you today. Is there anything I can do?" He quietly waited for her to look up so he could gauge how she was doing. His wolf growled softly as he sensed her unease.

She couldn't help but smile. "Thank you. But no, he'll give up eventually."

He almost couldn't breathe, she was so beautiful when she smiled. A smile, in his opinion, that could outshine the sun, and he was going to do whatever it took to make sure she was always happy from this day forward.

He decided a game might be a good way to learn a bit more about his lovely mate without stepping on any more landmines.

"How about we play a little game? I'll tell you something about me, and you tell me something about you."

V.A. Dold

She nodded and studied him expectantly, and waited to hear what he would tell her about himself.

"I'll start. I've lived here all my life. I've traveled extensively but never actually lived anywhere else."

"I was in Denver for the last fifteen years or so. I vacationed here about a dozen times over the years and fell in love with New Orleans. A dream came true when I was able to move here." She paused as if considering what she wanted to say next. "If you don't mind my asking, have you ever been married?" She instantly wanted to snatch the words back.

"I haven't, and I don't have any children yet. I don't have a girlfriend either so I guess that means we're both available, and this is our first date." He grinned broadly at Anna, turning on every ounce of charm he possessed.

She giggled and blushed a pretty pink. The sound was music to his ears.

He quickly asked another question, wanting to keep the lightness of the conversation going and ease her wariness. "Here's an easy one. My favorite color is green. Not light green or Kelly green, but a deep forest green."

She leaned forward. "Is it all right if I have two favorite colors?"

He gave her a smile and nodded. He felt like a teen on his very first date with the most popular girl in class.

"I like bright royal blue and deep purple," she said as she nodded as if she agreed with her choices. The movements made her hair shimmer in the sun. He hadn't noticed the intriguing golden highlights in the darkness of the bar.

37

Cade: Le Beau Brothers

"Do you have any brothers or sisters, Anna? I have six younger brothers." He let out a laugh as he recalled his childhood. "We had a very noisy house growing up."

"I have two older brothers, but I don't see them often. Our home was pretty loud, too. I can't even begin to imagine seven boys at once. Your mother must be an amazing woman."

He smiled as he thought of his family. "She is. She and my father are both incredible. I'm very lucky to have them."

The waitress approached again with their lunch and fresh drinks.

He glanced at Anna. "Do you prefer one dish over the other, or would you like to split both?"

*****

Two hours flew by, and the table had been cleared, leaving only Anna and Cade. With a resigned sigh, she pushed her chair back to stand and go.

Cade's hand shot out, and he gently grabbed her wrist.

Startled her eyes locked with his.

"Anna, may I walk you to your apartment or give you a ride home?" She heard a slight plea in his voice.

"Sure. I walked–it's not far."

What the heck am I saying, I may recognize him from the dreams, but realistically I just met this man.

After he had settled the bill, they exited onto Decatur Street and headed toward her place. As they walked, his fingers entwined with hers.

This is exactly like in my dreams; she smiled to herself. *I could get used to this.*

They reached her door much too soon for her liking. She paused, uncertain what to do.

Do I invite him in?

Give him a kiss?

Say thank you and goodbye?

He reached for her, searching her eyes. Slowly he pulled her toward him.

Oh, man. He's going to kiss me.

She felt his breath fan her cheek as he leaned in and stopped short. He held there…waiting.

Does he want me to kiss him?

Gathering her courage, she met him the rest of the way.

Oh, my gosh! His lips are so soft.

The kiss was sweet and gentle. He pulled away a few inches and hesitated before stepping back. "May I call you?"

"Yes, I'd love that." A thousand butterflies erupted in her stomach. "Come in and I'll write down my number."

Fumbling with her keys, she unlocked and opened the door. Quickly she grabbed a notepad sitting on a side table and scribbled her number with a shaky hand. She was so nervous; her writing looked like a second grader. Heat rose up her neck when she handed it to him.

As he reached for the scrap of paper, he made contact with her fingers causing a zing to run up his arm. Waiting until tomorrow to see her was not going to be an option–it would kill him.

"Would you have dinner with me tonight?"

Cade: Le Beau Brothers

"Really? I'd like that."

He heard a nervous quaver in her voice. She was absolutely adorable. He took the one step needed to reach her. Wrapping his arm around her waist, he paused for a pounding heartbeat, a chance to say no. She held her ground and licked her lip unconsciously. The glimpse of her little pink tongue made him want to growl.

Drawing her closer, he kissed her. More passionately with this second kiss. Enough to satisfy his wolf, but not too much. He didn't want to scare her away.

"Should I pick you up at seven?" He didn't want to keep her out too late on a work night.

"Seven is perfect," she whispered.

Cade squeezed her hand one last time and forced himself to leave. His wolf fought him all the way out the door.

Practically dancing down the sidewalk, he called the restaurant to secure them a table for 7:15 sharp.

He was getting the best table in the house. Due to owning businesses all over the city, everyone knew him in the Quarter, and he had no problem getting a reservation anywhere, anytime.

Excitement raced through him, and the next few hours were going to kill him.

*****

Cade knocked on her door at exactly seven pm, giving them plenty of time to reach the restaurant. His sweat–dampened fingers tugged at his stiff shirt collar while he waited for her to answer the door.

Anna came to the door in a clingy royal blue wrap dress.

Exquisite cleavage was his only thought before his brain stuttered to a halt.

She cleared her throat, calling his attention up to her eyes. "Hello."

His brain kicked back into gear. "Um... Hello. Are you ready?"

She laughed quietly. "Yes. I'll grab my sweater and lock up."

The view from behind was just as good as the front. He felt his slacks getting tight. The walk to the restaurant might be a bit uncomfortable.

They entered the restaurant a few minutes later, a blessedly short walk in his condition.

The young woman reviewing the reservation ledger at the maître d' stand greeted them. "May I help you?"

"Cade Le Beau," was all he said.

"Please follow me. We have your table waiting."

The hostess led them to a private table, overlooking the courtyard below. The view was spectacular.

He watched as Anna spent a few minutes looking at the lush tropical plants. A few were in bloom. She closed her eyes and breathed in deeply, prompting a small smile to play across her lips.

Anna's attention was drawn from the courtyard when the waiter came to their table. "Mr. Le Beau," the young man greeted. "How nice to see you tonight. Would you like to see a drink menu?"

Cade turned to Anna. "I usually get a wonderful red wine here. Would you like to try it, or do you prefer something else?"

"The wine sounds perfect."

After the waiter had left, Anna asked, "How often do you come here?"

"I don't know, once a week or so. I'm in the Quarter quite often, and this place is one of my favorites. I'm a bachelor, or at least I used to be." He gave her a lopsided grin and winked while taking her hand from across the table. "Eating at a good restaurant is pretty much essential to survival for single guys." He chuckled. "Most of us can't cook and we'd just starve." "Have you eaten here before?"

"I have, not as often as you, but I'm not a bachelor," she teased back. "I must say, their food is really good."

"I, for one, am very glad you aren't a bachelor," he laughed.

Anna looked back at her menu but must have felt his gaze on her. She flicked her eyes back to him. "What?"

He rested his chin on his hand and continued gazing, a slight grin to his lips. "What?" he asked back.

She leaned forward and whispered. "Why are you looking at me like that?"

"I can't help it. You look amazing," he whispered back.

She lowered her eyes to her lap, laughed and shook her head at his antics.

The waiter returned with the wine. "Are you ready to order?"

Cade looked at her. "I really like the blackened redfish and the shrimp creole. Would you like to share with me again?"

She smiled. "Déjà vu, just like lunch. Sounds yummy."

Cade handed him the menus and sat forward so he could take her hand again. "I may sound crazy, but you make me happy just by being with me." He caressed her hand gently like she was a fragile family heirloom.

*****

About halfway through their meal, the hostess passed the table leading another couple to the other end of the dining room. Anna glanced at them–it was her ex–husband, Tim, with a platinum blond in tight, revealing clothing.

She looks like a hooker, she thought.

Tim hesitated the instant he saw Anna.

She experienced a bit of satisfaction at the surprise on Tim's face at seeing her with such a handsome man.

Tim raked Anna with a sneer while his date openly drooled over Cade. The woman cleared her throat to get his attention. It didn't work.

Cade slowly stood, towering over Tim's five foot eight stature. As he glared at Tim, he took a deep breath, memorizing his scent.

Tim timidly sidestepped away from the perimeter of their table, avoiding getting too close.

Cade took his seat and turned back to Anna, looked deeply into her eyes and took her hand.

She was relieved there hadn't been a scene.

"That was my ex. Sorry about the interruption."

"Not a problem. Now I know who he is."

That was an interesting response. I wonder what he meant by it?

She watched him make a pretty good dent in the two dinners. He had a very healthy appetite. She paused from eating her redfish. "I would love to know your secret."

"What secret?" he frowned.

"How do you eat the way you do and stay so fit?"

He laughed. "I must have a fast metabolism. All my brothers eat as much as I do."

"Your parents must have had a huge grocery bill," she said, grinning.

"I imagine they did. I never really thought about it."

The rest of the meal was wonderful. He treasured every second with his mate.

Setting his empty wine glass on the table, he stood and helped her with her chair. "Have I told you how beautiful you are tonight?" he whispered in her ear.

"No, but thank you." Anna blushed again, and he secretly hoped the day would never come when she stopped blushing.

As they exited, Cade glanced toward Tim's table. The hair on the back of his neck stood on end. The table was empty.

Where has the little weasel gone?

He relished the walk back with Anna. The cool night breeze ruffled wisps of hair by her cheeks and gave her skin a light blush. A full moon added a shadowy glow to the street lamps' wattage. When she took his hand, his heart skipped a beat. His wolf howled joyfully at their mate's initiative. If only they had further to walk, like fifty miles.

Entering her courtyard, he caught Tim's scent. A VERY fresh scent. A low growl rumbled from his chest.

Anna stiffened.

He saw her trying to see into the shadows. His warning had startled her. He scanned the area but hadn't located Tim yet.

As she unlocked her door, she turned to him shyly. "Would you like to come in?"

"More than anything." He felt like he was grinning like a fool but didn't care. He had hoped she'd invite him in. He could make sure Tim wasn't inside, among 'other' possibilities.

She laughed. "You're so funny."

As they entered, he breathed deeply. Thankfully Tim's stench wasn't present.

"Would you like a drink?" she asked.

"I would love a beer if you have one."

Cade texted his brother, Stefan while Anna was getting their drinks.

Giving him Anna's address, he sent, *meet me at Anna's near the fountain.*

Settling on the couch, he patted the cushion next to him. "Come, sit by me."

As she joined him, he felt her body heat, like fingers searching for him. Taking her hand, he kissed the center of her palm before lacing his fingers with hers.

"Do you have a lot of work tomorrow?" he asked.

"I have one large project to present, so maybe a half day's work. How about you?"

"I'll be in town for meetings until after lunch, and then free the rest of the day. Would you like to spend the afternoon with me?"

"I would love to. Do you want me to meet you somewhere?"

"No, darling, my mother taught me to always go to a lady's door. I will come for you when you call to say you're ready." He leaned in and kissed her to make his point.

"Well, I certainly wouldn't go against your mother," she teased. "I had a wonderful time tonight, Cade. Thank you."

"I had a terrific evening as well. But I should say goodnight. You have a busy morning, and I'm keeping you up," he said. He gave her one last kiss and was gone.

As much as he wanted to stay forever, he needed to find out what Tim was up to. A nagging in his gut said Tim was coming back.

Tonight.

Chapter 4

Protecting Anna

Cade noted the fifth and eighth stair treads creaked. Security lighting was almost non-existent. Neighbor and foot traffic, also nil. To him, Anna was a sitting duck. Silently passing through the jungle in the courtyard, he approached Stefan downwind.

"Thank you for coming, Stefan."

"Always. What's going on?"

He brushed his fingers through his hair. "My mate was married before. Her ex-followed her here from Denver and has been harassing her. She told me about their history, and he sounds desperate and a bit unstable. I met him tonight. His scent became laced with aggression the moment he saw Anna. When I walked her to the door, his scent was everywhere. He had lingered outside her door for quite a while. I believe he may come back tonight."

"Not good. Desperation makes a person do stupid things. What do you want me to do?"

"I'll stay in the shadows in the alcove near her door. You stay out of sight down here watching for him to come through the courtyard." Cade tilted his head toward the staircase. "Go to her door and get his scent, then we'll take our positions."

He stepped into the shadows as he waited for Stefan.

"The man reeks of deception," his brother said when he returned, his nose wrinkled in disgust.

"I agree. If you see him coming, signal, but let him pass. I need him to go into her apartment. I can't take action against him without cause. I won't give Anna any reason to doubt my intentions."

"If I'm going to let him pass, why do you need me?"

"To stop me from killing him."

"Good point."

"All right. Go wolf. You will be less noticeable."

Cade was a whisper as he made his way to the alcove, skipping stairs five and eight, then disappearing into the shadows.

For almost an hour, only the occasional dog barking in the distance broke the silence. Then he heard a creak; a heartbeat later, another. Cade saw Stefan's signal and remained completely invisible to Tim.

A door handle jiggled in the silence, then scratching of metal on metal. Tim turned the knob and entered.

Cade was inside in a flash, two steps behind Tim, not making a sound. If the moron threatened his mate, he was in a position to act. He needed Anna to wake and catch Tim in her apartment if he wanted any hope of her leaving with him tonight. He knew she wouldn't agree any other way. She didn't see Tim as the danger he presented.

They neared her sleeping form, and a few heartbeats passed before Tim extended his hands toward her throat. The instant skin contacted skin; Cade struck.

Anna screamed long and loud. The bedside lamp crashed to the floor as she fumbled to light the room.

Stefan joined Cade in the apartment the instant he saw him move from the alcove. With a flick of the light switch by the door, the room was alive with light.

Anna scrambled, flattening herself against the headboard. Her eyes shot to Cade holding Tim prone on the floor. "What ...Why..."

"Stefan, I'm going to let this idiot up. If he moves, take him down."

Cade reached for his mate cowering in her bed. Her eyes wide and brows pulled tight, tracked him as he approached. "May I sit with you, cher?"

She scooted over, her eyes never leaving his.

"I caught Tim breaking into your apartment. He was wrapping his hands around your throat."

She leaned forward to see her ex. Her expression melted into a dark scowl. "Are you insane!?" she yelled at Tim.

Sneering, Tim said, "Who is this?" pointing at Cade and raking him up and down like he actually thought he could take him.

She raised her chin higher in defiance. "That's none of your business. I should call the police and have you arrested."

Tim bristled. "I don't want a strange man in your apartment. He needs to leave. Now."

She scooted around Cade and stood almost nose–to–nose with her ex. She narrowed her eyes before she said, much too quietly, "No, Tim, YOU need to leave. Preferably leave the entire state. Why did you move here anyway?"

Cade flexed his shoulders, deliberately allowing a visible ripple of muscle under his skin–tight, white t–shirt. To the human world, he strove to be a perfect gentleman, but actually he was a lethal predator when the need arose. Tim needed to know how dangerous he was, in no uncertain terms. He was like a dog rising slowly, menacingly, with its hackles raised and canines displayed in a vicious snarl.

Anna shook her head and turned to leave the room. Tim snatched her by the arm and swung her around.

An ominous snarl from Cade made her jump, and before Tim knew what hit him, he was face down on the floor with the hand he dared to touch Cade's mate with twisted behind his back.

Painfully, and at an unnatural angle.

Tim screamed like a little girl and began to cry from the pain of his now broken arm. Anna covered her mouth to hide a grin. She felt a little bad about actually being happy Tim had gotten his due and karma had just bit him in the ass.

Cade glanced at her. "Cher, what would you like me to do with this trash? Do you want me to hold him here while you call the police?"

She gave Tim a good, long look. She was rather enjoying him whimpering on the floor. With one last dismissive glance, she said, "No, I prefer to not tell my children I put their father in prison, regardless of how much he's earned his orange jumpsuit. I'll file a restraining order against him tomorrow."

Cade wasn't happy about her ex running loose, but he saw her point. "All right. The police will need a statement about tonight to give cause."

"Okay. Give me a couple minutes to call them," she said.

"Do you want me to hang around?" Stefan asked.

"No, I have this. Thanks for coming."

Stefan gave him a mock salute and left.

Moments later her voice floated in from the living room as she called 9–1–1. Within minutes, sirens blared in the distance, and then footsteps of several police officers pounded in the courtyard.

Cade held Tim on the floor until the first officer entered the bedroom. In instances like this, it was nice to know all the officers in New Orleans personally. "Good evening, Al."

"Hello, Cade. What's the situation here?"

He dug his knee into Tim's back as he stood. The added pressure caused Tim to scream like a little girl again.

Al jerked him off the floor and slapped cuffs on him, eliciting another howl.

"This is the ex–husband of Anna James, the woman who lives here. He broke in and was reaching for her neck as she slept when I disabled him. Anna would like to get a restraining order on him tomorrow. Will you be able to push through the report tonight?"

Al glared at Tim. "Absolutely."

"Also, please have the judge draw up the strictest restraining order available and deliver it to her."

"Consider it done."

Minutes later, Tim was riding to the station in the back of a squad.

*****

"Cher, are you okay? You're trembling."

"Yes. It's just rather terrifying to wake up with a man standing over you. He's never acted like a crazy person before."

Taking her hand, he led her to the couch. "Let me hold you." As he comforted her, he quietly hummed a love song from long ago.

"You have a wonderful voice." When he ended the song, she snuggled closer to his chest. "Thank you for coming back."

"I will always protect you, cher. Since we're on that subject, we need to talk."

She sat straighter to see his face. "All right."

"You're not safe here with him on the loose, even with a restraining order. I'm not sure what his game is—yet—but I'll find out. In the meantime, I would like you to stay in a hotel where he can't find you. In a public place with lots of people."

"You're right. After tonight, I don't want to stay here. What do you have in mind?"

"Pack a bag and I'll take you to a hotel on Canal Street."

"Okay. Give me a minute, and we can leave."

*****

Fifteen minutes later, they entered the lobby, and he went directly to the registration desk and asked for the manager. She was confused.

What the heck is he doing? You don't need the manager to get a room.

Within moments, the manager came from the back. He took one look at Cade and a huge smile broke across his face. "Cade! It's wonderful to see you. What brings you in tonight?"

"Hello, Miles." He reached out and shook his friend's hand. "I'd like a suite for the lady here for at least three nights, possibly a little longer, while we find her a place to stay."

Miles tapped keys on the computer keyboard and handed him two key cards. "Suite 2615 is all yours for as long as you need. Just drop off the keys when you're ready to check out. No rush, no charge."

She was floored. Did he actually just get her a free suite for an unlimited time? Good grief, she needed to learn more about this man. They rode the elevator in silence. She was unsure how to even begin the conversation currently running through her mind.

He walked her to the door, and he held it open, allowing her to step in first.

She entered and took a look around the HUGE two–room suite. The space was a combination of a large room with a wet bar, eight–person oak dining room table and living room to seat at least six with a sixty–inch flat screen. Through a door on the other end of the room was a bedroom with a king–size bed. The suite was larger than her two–bedroom apartment.

She sat on the couch and stared at her feet as she decided what to say.

"Don't get me wrong. I appreciate everything you've done, but why are you doing this for me? I'm a complete stranger you just met. I'm not used to people making grand gestures like you have. To be honest, it makes me nervous."

Cade: Le Beau Brothers

He searched for the best way to answer. Maybe the romance novel torture inflicted by his cousin when he was young could be useful here. A lot of women read romance novels, according to Julia. This was worth a shot as a lead–in.

His younger cousin, who eats, sleeps, and breathes romance novels, really gets a kick out of the shifter ones. He shook his head thinking about her book addiction. Regardless, she tormented all her male cousins with endless renditions of her latest favorite read. The boys were spoon–fed romance novels ad nauseam. Because of the experience, he had become an unwilling expert in romance novel trivia.

He took the opening she offered, deciding there was no time like the present. With his heart racing, he took a chance.

"Cher, do you like to read?"

She stared at him like he was a crazy person. "What?"

What does reading have to do with this hotel room?

"Do you like to read? For example, have you ever read romance novels?"

Crud, she thinks I'm a complete nutcase.

Her brow furrowed, and she seemed confused by his questions. "Yes…Why?"

He held up his hands more in a pleading gesture than defeat. "Please, bear with me, okay? Have you read any paranormal romance books?"

She let a little grin escape as she answered, "Yes. Would you like to borrow one? I brought a few with me when I moved here."

He gave her a crooked grin and cleared his throat.

"No, that won't be necessary. Have you ever read one with shifters? Like men who can change into wolves?"

"Yes, I've read many of them. A lot of them take place here in New Orleans. Those are my favorite."

Taking a deep breath again, he mentally encouraged himself.

Come on, Cade, you can do this. Take the chance–she seems open to the possibility.

Anna jumped up and stared wide-eyed. She took a couple of steps back and sidestepped behind the couch, placing it like a protective barrier between them.

With her voice shaking slightly, she asked him, "Did I just hear your thoughts?"

He studied her face. "Yes. I'm sure you did."

Her hand covered her mouth as she gasped in shock. She stood frozen, unable to take her eyes off him. Afraid to move, although why moving would make a difference she had no idea. He wasn't a T–Rex, for crying out loud.

He directed another thought to her.

Cher, don't be afraid. Please sit and let me explain why I'm talking about romance books and why you are hearing me in your head.

She didn't speak right away. She just stood across the room trembling.

She was both curious and a little leery. Here was her fantasy man who in her dreams turned into a wolf, asking her about reading paranormal romances. With her curiosity winning out, she wanted to see where he was going with this.

An expression flickered over her face as if she'd made her decision. He watched her slowly lower her hand and take a deep breath, then straighten her shoulders. She seemed to be gathering courage as she walked around the couch and took a seat.

He remained quiet and watched the expressions flit across his mate's face. He wanted to give her time to digest the fact she could hear his thoughts. Once she appeared to have relaxed a bit, he started again. "You may be wondering if you can speak to me as well. The answer is yes."

Her eyes got wide again. "Please tell me you can't read ALL my thoughts! That would be so embarrassing."

He chuckled. "No, you have to be thinking very loudly without walls or barriers for me to hear your thoughts. Otherwise, I'll only hear what you direct to me specifically." He found his mate more and more entertaining.

She let out a sigh. "Good. Who would want another person in their head all the time? Ugh, the thought is horrifying."

He cocked his head. "Would you like to try? All you have to do is think something directly at me."

She considered what to ask for a moment and then thought at him, *what are my favorite colors?*

He grinned broadly and thought back, *bright royal blue and deep purple.*

Anna gasped, and her grin became huge.

He was relieved she was enjoying this and not running for the door. He'd managed a minor hurdle. Now for a REALLY BIG one. "Let's continue with the shifter stories. Do you believe they could exist, and people simply don't know about them?" He held his breath waiting for her response.

Hold on! Why is he asking me about them being real? Could he actually be the man from my dreams? He looks like him, has the same voice, and in my dreams I made him a wolf. Or did I? Was I really in control of those dreams? She gasped as the possibility hit her. *What if they are real and he IS one!*

She grabbed a throw pillow lying next to her on the couch and hugged it in front of her as though the satin and fill would somehow shield her from danger. "I need to ask you something, but you're going to think I'm crazy."

"I would never think that. Go ahead and ask me anything."

She braced herself and just spit it out. "I've been having dreams about a man exactly like you for the past five years. And right before I met you at the bar I was daydreaming about him...you...whatever." She blushed profusely but forged on. "Why have I been dreaming about you when we'd never met? Have you been projecting these dreams into my head somehow?"

"Anna, I've been having dreams and visions of you for the past five years as well, and I had a vision of you right before I walked into the bar." He stopped as if organizing his thoughts. "I think I know what's happening. In mine, I was cupping your face and kissing you when suddenly the dream disappeared."

She clutched the pillow tighter. "I was having the exact same dream, right before you walked up to me."

He rubbed his jaw. "I don't think we're dreaming at all. I think somehow we've been sharing these experiences in our minds. Somehow we're actually there, and everything in our dreams is real, that it is all, in fact, happening."

Cade: Le Beau Brothers

He saw her confusion. She must have been wondering how they could have been sharing experiences with their minds. This kind of thing didn't happen to humans. And yet it had.

He leaned forward with his elbows on his knees in as much of a relaxed posture as he could muster. His wolf was growling at him for frightening their mate. He really had to rein in this situation before it went sideways on him. If ever there was a time for a dose of Cajun charm, this was it.

"Cher, I don't mean to frighten you. I'm trying to tell you something without upsetting you. Believe me, there is nothing to be afraid of. I'd never let anything harm you. Let's go back to what I was talking about with the shifters. I think this will all be explained as we go."

Anna let out the breath she was holding as she pieced her thoughts together.

Do I believe they could be real? Yeah. I mean who really knows what all is out there?

With a little hesitation, she tried to keep her voice from shaking too badly.

"Sure, I think there are a lot of things humans have no knowledge of. New things come to light every day. I have never met one that I know of, but yeah, it could be possible." Then she sat back and waited for him to shift into a wolf.

She watched Cade closely. He was in deep thought as though deciding something very important. When he didn't change into a wolf and remained quiet, she started to wonder what he was trying to tell her.

After what seemed like forever, she sighed. "Whatever it is, just say it."

Raking his fingers through his hair, he took another deep breath. "Please tell me you'll remain calm and keep an open mind?"

She studied him expectantly. "Okay, I'll try."

Oh, man, here it comes. He's going to change like in my dreams.

Nothing. No, wolf.

Really? That's it? She frowned at him crossing her arms. W*hat the heck?*

Finally, he said, "You've officially met a shifter."

Huh? Maybe he isn't one after all. Maybe he means someone else I met is a shifter.

Her brows scrunched as she gazed across the room into nothingness, trying to remember when she might have met someone who could be a shifter.

Throwing her hands up in the air, she gave up and turned back to him. "Who? When did I meet one?"

He smiled at her and held out his arms wide to her as if welcoming her in. "Me, cher, I'm a shifter."

She gaped at him for a moment. "Well, that was sure anticlimactic. Are you telling me the truth, or are you completely nuts?"

He rubbed his chin as though considering that. "If I shift only my right arm, will that prove it to you? You won't completely freak out, right?"

The idea of seeing him change actually excited her.

It would be awesome if he really was one and shifting would sure be one way to prove it.

Finally, she nodded her agreement.

He appeared concerned. "Okay, you ready? I don't want to scare you."

She nodded again, and in the blink of an eye, his right arm was now the foreleg of a wolf with a paw.

She sat in amazement for a moment. Then, without thinking, she reached out and stroked the now wolf foreleg. He actually moaned in ecstasy, and his wolf rumbled in satisfaction at his mate's stroking. She quickly pulled her hand back, and he practically whimpered at the loss of her touch.

"You really are a shifter," Anna whispered to herself.

Chapter 5

What is a Mate?

Cade gave her a few minutes to regroup after everything he'd thrown at her in the last fifteen minutes. Once he was satisfied she would be ready for the main revelation, he began again. "Cher, please, look at me." He waited for her to give him her full attention. "May I please sit with you on the couch?"

She scooted over and made room for him next to her. Then she watched him as he moved from the chair to sit with her.

What does wolf man have up his sleeve now? She thought smiling.

Her bad pun made him chuckle. He sat, turned toward her, and then slowly reached out and took her hands in his.

Cade searched her eyes and scented the air for signs of distress, and having found none, he began. "Cher, when a shifter finds his one true mate, there are specific signs to alert him that she's the one."

When she remained silent with an attentive expression, he continued. "He'll be unnaturally drawn to her and she'll have a scent designed specifically to attract only him, just as he will have a scent specifically for her." As he said this, he took a deep breath as if he were breathing her in.

"When he hears her voice, the experience will be like he is being knocked off his feet and the world opens for him in new, brighter, more fantastic ways."

Her brow furrowed. But before she asked any questions, he carried on.

"The sensation is very hard to describe, but when a shifter experiences it, what he feels is very dramatic and undeniable. And there's one last and all–defining proof that a shifter has found his mate." Cade gazed deeply into her eyes. "He'll hear her thoughts and she will hear his."

He heard her gasp and saw her frantically searching his face with her eyes.

Then he heard her voice in his mind as she pleaded,

Please don't break my heart, Cade.

Her thought hit him like a battering ram and tore his heart out. The last thing he would ever do on this Earth would be to hurt her in any way.

He leaned in close to her ear and whispered, "Mate, I will never break your heart. Ever. You are the other half of my soul, my reason for living." He pulled back searching her face.

Her eyes took on a bright sparkle, and he heard her heart pounding wildly.

Then her thoughts came loud and clear; *This is really happening... To me! The man of my dreams is real... AND... He's a freaking shifter. AND somehow I'm his mate. Holy cow!*

He lowered his face slowly toward her but stopped a breath away from touching. She closed the distance, and he brushed his mouth softly against hers. His breath fanned gently over her skin raising goose bumps in its wake.

Running his tongue along the seam of her lips, he requested entrance. She leaned into him; her hands gripped his shoulders in a way a person might hold onto a life raft. Her soft curves pressed against his chest and abdomen, the sensation made him want to growl in ecstasy.

She sighed, and her lips parted. That was all he needed, and he deepened the kiss. His tongue dove inside caressing and memorizing every dip, every curve. Tightening his arms around her, he took away any chance of Anna escaping. He wanted his kiss to show her she was everything to him. His hands slid through her hair and cupped the back of her head as their bodies molded together perfectly.

He felt her letting go and accepting him, but he didn't want her to mistakenly view this as only sex. This was too important to screw up. He slowly broke away. Leaning his forehead against hers, breathing heavily, he gathered his control again. With one last nuzzle to her neck, he inhaled her scent into his lungs and leaned away from her.

"I'm sorry. I didn't mean to take liberties. Are you all right?"

She nodded in answer but didn't speak. Before he could become worried by her silence, he heard her thoughts.

Cade: Le Beau Brothers

Holy cow, his kiss completely jumbled my brain. I have never been kissed so completely before. This man is dangerous to women everywhere with a kiss like that.

Her whole body tingled. She'd never been kissed like she was the most important person to anyone before. Like she was adored. Wanted. Desired.

He wrapped his arms around her and drew her close. His wolf sighed in relief, to finally hold his mate. The peace Anna gave them simply by sharing herself this way was profound. After a few minutes, he relaxed his hold on her, and, cupping the side of her face, waited for her to look at him. "Do you have any questions you would like to ask?"

She had so many questions running around in her brain she wasn't sure where to begin. She had smelled the wonderful, warm chocolate and fresh baked bread in the restaurant, and the delicious fragrance surrounded her again. The aroma must be what he was talking about for a special scent.

Finally, she settled on one. "What exactly does being a mate mean?"

He nodded his head. "That's a fair question. To be a mate is to be married, but so much more. We were created to complete each other. You hold the other half of my soul and I yours. Literally. Only by performing the mating ritual will our soul be knit back together to form our complete soul. Prior to meeting me, did you ever feel odd, incomplete, like there was something missing, but you couldn't put your finger on what?"

Anna nodded yes. "Now that you mention it, I did feel odd and out of place like I never really belonged. A lot. I never knew what was missing, and I could never find anything or anyone to make the feeling go away. I've always felt different like I didn't fit in with other people."

She took a moment to consider her next question. "If we do the mating ritual, will I be able to shift, too?" She couldn't help the anticipation in her voice.

I really, really hope I'll be able to shift. That would be so cool!

He grinned at her. "Yes. Yes, you will. I personally can't wait to meet your sexy wolf, and my wolf is howling inside with his excitement."

She laughed with delight and peered up at him. Then she blushed as she thought about the rest of what he had said. "Really?" she asked shyly.

I can't believe he thinks anything about me is sexy. I'm obviously older than him, and he doesn't have an ounce of fat on him. Not like me.

She saw him scowl at her. He pulled her close again and buried his face in her hair. "Really. I don't like the less than flattering thoughts you often have about yourself." He breathed into her ear. "You're the sexiest woman I've ever met."

You'd be surprised how old I really am. And I love your curves, they turn me on. Remember how your luscious body drove me crazy in our visions?

Her heart skipped a beat at his words. She was both excited and a little shy about the memories of what they'd done together in the visions. She was so distracted she almost forgot to ask her next question. "Will I be changed at all when we mate? In the movies, the human is bitten and becomes a werewolf. What will happen to me?"

Cade cocked his head much like a wolf or dog

would. "Yes and no. You'll have a long life. Shifters live to be around fourteen hundred years old. I was born in eighteen hundred three. I'm actually two hundred ten years old. We aren't immortal, but we do live a very long time. I believe because of our aging process, you'll get younger at this point. I guess the best word for this type of conversion is regression. At maturity a shifter appears to be around twenty–five to thirty years old, and they remain looking the same age until they are about nine hundred years old, and then they begin to very slowly age again. So you'll appear the same as you did in your mid–twenties and have the features you had then."

She paused for a moment as though she were considering what he had just told her.

WOW! Being younger again would be so cool, I'd love to look like I'm twenty–five again! I wonder if everything becomes younger. I passed the age line for having children a couple years ago. Will that regress as well?

She stared at the floor and blushed a pretty shade of pink as she asked, "When I regress, will my female parts, the reproductive parts to be exact, get younger again as well?"

He tried to remember if he had ever heard of any wolf having a mate regress who was beyond childbearing years before and what would happen.

I should call my mother on this one to verify everything.

Not wanting to give his mate false information he said, "Give me a minute to make a call about having children. I'm not sure, and I want to give you an honest answer."

V.A. Dold

She took the chance to excuse herself. As she was returning, he was ending the call.

He gave her a huge smile. "Yes, actually, you'll regress in every way and be able to have children if you so desire."

Her heart leapt. She had always wanted more children. Now she would have the chance to love another baby and watch him or her grow up. Cade's baby!

"Would you please explain to me exactly what the ritual is? I mean what do we have to do?" She was a bit worried that the process of changing might really hurt. Like, hurt a lot. In some of those werewolf movies, shifting seemed really painful.

"There are actually several parts to the ritual. First there is the request, where I ask you formally if you will give yourself to me to make me complete. The mating goes like this:

'Will you give yourself, body and soul, to complete this man and his wolf?

'Will you unite your life with mine, bond your future with mine, and merge your half of our soul to mine, and in doing so complete the mating ritual?'

"The second part is your formal response, which is:

'I will give myself, body and soul, to complete you as a man and a wolf.

'I will unite my life with yours, bond my future to yours, and merge my half of our soul with yours.

'I will complete the mating ritual with you.'

"Then as we join our bodies together and make love, I make my vow to you, which is:

'I claim you as my mate.

67

Cade: Le Beau Brothers

'I belong to you as you belong to me.

'I give you my heart and my body.

'I will protect you even with my life.

'I give you all I am.

'I share my half of our soul to complete you.

'I share my magic with you.

'I beseech the great Luna Goddess to bless you and your wolf guardian.

'You are my mate to cherish today and for all time.

'I claim you as my mate.'

"At the part where I say I share my magic with you, I bite you right here, where your neck and shoulder meet. But don't worry, this won't be painful. I'm told my bite will be quite erotic.

"Then you say those same words to me and bite me in the same manner.

"That's the complete ritual."

She gazed at him, wonder in her eyes. "So there won't be anything painful?"

He broke out laughing. "No, Cher, there's no pain."

Standing, he took her by the hand and led her to the bedroom.

"We've both had a tough night. May I hold you? I will remain fully clothed if that makes you more comfortable." As he searched her eyes, he reached out and caressed her cheek with the back of his fingers, drinking her in.

"I want you to stay with me. I feel safe when you're with me. I don't want to be alone," she said quietly.

They snuggled on the bed fully clothed. Completely relaxed for the first time since they had arrived, he wrapped his arms around her. Tucked her as close as he could get her, and just cuddled.

Within minutes, he heard a soft snore, and when he lifted his head, he found she was fast asleep.

Chapter 6

Courting Anna

Cade thought he was dreaming as he slowly woke with his mate in his arms. Smiling to himself, he pulled her close. He relished the feel of her curves pressed against him.

Yawning, she started to wake. He felt her wiggle as she rose from her sleepy haze. No doubt, unaware the thing that hindered her movements was him.

Cade loosened his hold so she could see him and get her bearings.

He knew the moment she was fully awake. Her eyes became as large as saucers, and she ran her hand down her body verifying that she was fully dressed. Her sigh of relief had him chuckling.

"Good morning, sunshine," he whispered as he kissed her thoroughly.

Breathing heavily, she said back, "Good morning," then yawned again. "Did last night really happen?"

"Sadly, yes, it did. Your restraining order will be delivered today."

"How did you manage that?" she asked frowning.

"I know the judge." He winked. "He's rushing the process for me as a favor."

"Do you know every single person who lives in this town?" She laughed.

"I'm sure there are one or two I haven't met yet," he teased. "I'll start the coffee. See you in a minute."

In the kitchenette, he started the pot and texted his brother. He needed clothes if he was going to stay with his mate and protect her.

Anna walked into the room wearing her bathrobe as she went for the first batch of coffee, then shuffled toward the couch.

Picking up his cup, he joined her in the living room to plan their day.

"I made sure when you were packing last night that your laptop was included. You said you had some work to do this morning,"

She sighed. "Thank you. I was so stressed I'm sure I would have forgotten it."

"I have my meeting in an hour. Once you're done working, please call me, and I'll finish up the meeting if it hasn't ended already. We have a date," he reminded her with a wink.

She smiled as she finished her cup and rose to get ready for the day.

Stefan arrived loaded with luggage as Cade heard the shower start in the next room. "How is she doing this morning?"

"Better than you would expect. She's handling everything extremely well."

"Does she know about you yet?"

He grinned to himself. "Yes, I told her last night."

Cade: Le Beau Brothers

Stefan's eyebrows disappeared into his hairline. "So, have you completed the ritual already?"

"No, I'm giving her time to process everything."

"Understandable. I have to go; I'm running late. Have a great day," he grinned at his brother as he walked out the door.

"Thanks again, Stefan, for everything."

They were both ready for the day, and, reluctantly, he had to get going if he was to make the meeting on time. Taking her lovely face in his hands, he gave her a light kiss. "I need to go. Have a great morning, cher." He gave her one last quick kiss on the way out the door.

*****

The past three hours felt like it had taken a week off his life. He checked his phone for the hundredth time.

Did time suddenly slow to a crawl?

He was ready to call Anna, unable to wait any longer when his phone rang.

Thank Goddess.

A thrill rushed through his chest. "Hello, cher."

"Hi, I'm finished for the day."

"Perfect. I will be right there," he said.

He ran the three blocks to the hotel. He couldn't wait to see her again.

Within minutes, he had her in the sunshine strolling down the block. She smiled brightly at him as he took her hand. Just having her hand in his made his heart race.

The foot traffic on the sidewalks was light today making it easy to walk side by side. Most days there were so many people, you had to dodge others constantly. Her eyes were a bright, happy green today and sparkled each time he glanced her way.

He raised her hand to his lips and placed a gentle kiss on the back of it as they walked.

She gave him a sweet smile in return. "I really like it when you do that. No one has ever kissed my hand before."

"Then I shall endeavor to kiss it more often," he teased.

"How did your meeting go?"

"Excellent. I'm reviewing one of our businesses. I needed to decide if we will retain it or sell. I was able to make some logistical adjustments, which should allow us to see a profit in about six months. How was your morning'?"

"Great. I pitched my campaign to the board. They agreed to my plan as a whole so I will move forward with the project next week."

"I would love to see your work. I find your mind fascinating." He gave her hand a little squeeze. He was so proud of her. "Yesterday you mentioned your sons. Have they come to visit since you moved here?"

"Not yet. We've talked about it, but they are staying so busy with new cases they haven't been able to spare the time," she said quietly.

"You must miss them." He brushed his thumb across the back of her hand to comfort her.

"Terribly." She gave him a small smile.

"Well, I hope they can visit soon," he said. "What would you like to do today?"

"I haven't been to the Frenchman's Market in a while. Would you like to walk there and stroll the booths? There are a few things I need to look for."

"I would love to." He would go anywhere with her.

Right then, his phone vibrated announcing a new email. Glancing, he saw it was from the courthouse. "Excuse me. I think I should check this."

Tim had been released after being visited by every officer on duty. They told Tim he was being watched, and he would not fare as well next time. The restraining order was attached.

"Is everything okay?" she asked.

He took a deep breath. "Tim has been released and I have a copy of your restraining order." He heard her heart rate increase.

She sucked in a breath. "I knew this was coming. It shouldn't surprise me," she sighed.

"You're safe, cher. He can't get near you as long as you're with me."

She nodded, trembling.

His wolf snarled. No one was allowed to terrorize their mate. Cade remained quiet, waiting for her to initiate more conversation.

She took a deep breath. "I won't let him dictate my life again. Thank you for taking care of the police and judge."

"My pleasure," he said forcefully.

Flowing with the other pedestrians on the sidewalk, they strode along. There was no rush, and she savored the feel of his hand holding hers. She felt like she could absorb his warmth and strength through that link.

The breeze ruffled her hair sending wisps into her eyes as they moved from one merchant to the next. Brushing it back, she looked through the purses on display.

A rack of leather belts caught her eye. "I could use a new brown belt," she told him as she looked through the different styles and lengths.

He joined her at the booth. "I think this one would be attractive on you," he said as he held it up for her.

She took it from him, turning it over in her hands and testing the length for fit. "I love it," she said smiling at him.

"Then it's yours," he grinned.

She worked her way from one end of the market to the other sharing an occasional find with Cade. Standing at the exit, she checked her watch. "Holy cow, we spent two hours here."

"Time flies when you're having fun," he laughed.

Yawning she said. "I must not have slept well last night. Do you mind if we go back to the hotel? I'd like a quick nap."

He gave her a dramatic bow. "Your wish is my command."

She laughed at him. "Come on, silly man."

"Let's hire one of the rickshaw bikes to take us back," he suggested. "It's a long walk."

"Great idea." She was really dragging, and a ride would be welcome.

The biker flew like the wind. She was surprised how fast he got them to the hotel. As she reached the bedroom, she literally fell into the bed and was asleep instantly.

Cade: Le Beau Brothers

Refreshed from her nap, she walked to the living room to find Cade working on his laptop.

"How are you feeling?" he asked holding his hand out to her.

"Much better. The stress really wiped me out." She checked the time, uncertain how long she slept. "Wow, I must have been really tired. I was out for hours," she exclaimed.

"You needed it," he said as he pulled her into his lap.

"Babe, can I ask you something that's been nagging at me?" she asked.

"You can ask me anything."

She turned to him. "You said you live fourteen hundred years. How do people not notice that?"

"It's a combination of the magic which allows us to appear to age for the benefit of humans as well as making people believe we are our own descendants. After a normal human lifetime, a descendant inherits the property and investments we have. Of course, this person is actually just us pretending to be our own relatives."

She thought about Cade pretending to be someone else. "So, have you had to change your name to be this new relative?"

He smiled, his eyes showing his pride and approval of her. "I knew you were a bright lady. The last name I used was Herbert."

She busted out laughing. "You don't look like a Herbert."

He laughed right along with her. "We can also move away for two or three decades and then come back. By time anyone who'd recognize our younger selves easily believes we are a child or nephew of the person they knew long ago."

She became very quiet and then asked in barely a whisper, "What do I do about my boys? I can't leave them and never see them again. I don't know if I can bear to watch them die."

His heart was breaking. He couldn't make this better for her with his magic. There were only two ways for her sons to join her in this new life, and both were very slim chances.

"I'm sorry to tell you the odds are great you'll outlive your human children. Without a shifter mate to share her magic with them, they'll only have a normal lifespan. The only positive to the situation is you would normally die when they are sixty or so, but now, even though you will outlive them, you'll be able to see them in their golden years."

He paused, trying to decide if he wanted to tell her about the other slim–to–none option. He didn't want to raise her hopes just to have her heart shattered later. His head dropped in defeat. As her mate, he couldn't keep anything from her. Without looking up, he spoke so softly she almost didn't hear him. "There is one other possibility. The chances of it happening are about the same as winning the lottery."

He felt her hand take his, and could tell by her lack of exhale that she was holding her breath.

"My mother is very powerful. She is known to speak with the wolf–Goddess on occasion. The Goddess is the original creator of the wolf shifters. Long ago, she blessed a village of humans with wolf souls. They were the first shifters. Since then, she has only blessed a handful of humans that were not mated to a born shifter. I could ask my mother to petition the Goddess on behalf of your sons. There's only a slim chance she would honor the request."

With a tear sliding down her cheek, she lifted her chin, expressing a strength he knew would always astonish him.

"Thank you for being honest with me. I'll think about the petition. I can't make a decision like that for them. That's something they would have to want."

They snuggled on the couch. The ease she felt with him was what you would expect from two people who had been together a long time. They were so comfortable with each other she almost giggled.

Apparently we have been, through our freaky connection.

She reached out, taking his hand into hers, and stroked his knuckles with her thumb. After a minute or two, she gazed up at him and leaned in, inviting him to kiss her with her body language. He took the hint, gently brushing her lips with his. The kiss started soft and slow, but the heat built quickly. Cade pulled her closer tasting her with his tongue. She mimicked his every move; all the while her fingertips stroked and explored his torso and chest. The kiss deepened; tongues tangled and slid seductively across each other.

He used his left palm to cradle her head as his right stroked up her ribcage over her shirt. He gently cupped her breast, rubbing his thumb back and forth across her hardened nipple. Both were breathing heavily as their hands roamed freely.

Like a driver slamming on the brakes, Anna sighed happily and got up, giving him a bit of a sassy grin. His agonized expression almost made her giggle.

She had to keep a straight face if this was going to work. The plan was to get him to take their real life affair to the next level, and the shower was a good place to do it.

"I think I'll take a shower now and wash this day away. Too bad you already took one…" she let her comment hang in the air.

As she left the room, she stole a come–hither glance at him over her shoulder.

I wonder if I gave a strong enough hint.

Pulling back the shower curtain, she turned on the water, testing the temperature with her fingertips. As she turned her back to the spray, she let out a groan of pleasure. The water beat down on her sore muscles and washed away the stress and tension of the day.

Maybe he isn't coming. I must not do sexy innuendos very well.

So, my mate can be a playful tease. Hmmm. He thought.

He gave her a minute to get settled into the shower, and then followed her silently with a sly grin on his face. Time to test the waters so to speak with his mate. He quietly walked into the bathroom and reached into the shower stealing away her shampoo. Now all he had to do was wait.

She had her eyes closed as she wet her hair in preparation. With eyes still closed, she reached out for the bottle she set on the ledge right before closing the curtain. Nothing. Anna patted around looking for the errant bottle with her fingers. Failing to find her shampoo, she cracked one eye open to see why. She let out a squeak in surprise.

Cade: Le Beau Brothers

As she tried to cover herself, he sensed her sudden, irrational, insecurity. It made no sense, but there it was, rearing its ugly head.

He ignored her thoughts for now, he would deal with her insecurities in a minute. Peeking around the curtain with the missing shampoo in his hand, he waggled the bottle back and forth just out of her reach with hunger in his eyes. "I can help you with that."

She giggled at the boyish expression on his face. He looked so hopeful. She hesitantly nodded her head and made room for him.

He didn't need to be invited twice. He zapped off his clothes and joined his mate so fast she almost stumbled backward into the faucet handles. In a flash, his hands whipped out to steady her before she was bruised in any way.

Her eyes almost popped out of her head! "How the heck did you make your clothes disappear?!"

"All you have to do is think it and it happens. With a little practice, you'll be able to do it, too, once we are mated and I share my magic with you."

He leaned her back into the warm spray from the showerhead to re–dampen her hair and massaged in her favorite shampoo. After rinsing her hair completely and applying the conditioner she used, he picked up the bar of Dove soap she preferred and lathered his hands. His wolf was giddy with the anticipation of sliding soapy hands all over his mate.

Anna stood with the warm spray to her back as he started at her shoulders soaping and massaging, making sure to clean every inch of her. He slowly washed her breasts, kneading, and caressing. He licked his lips in anticipation as he rubbed his thumbs across her hardened nipples. Reluctantly, he left her breasts, proceeding over her stomach to her thighs not missing a single bit of her succulent flesh. Relishing every bit of her.

She held out her hand for the soap and bathed him just as thoroughly. The feel of his rock hard chest and abdomen seemed to fascinate her. Slowly she soaped his washboard stomach, making him breathe heavily. She applied more soap to her hands, and before he knew what she intended, she had both hands wrapped around his rock hard erection. He let out a low moan as she stroked him with her slick grip.

There was no way he was going to be able to take more of her stimulation and still be able to help with her shower. And he had every intention of washing her thoroughly. He stilled her hands and placed them at her sides. Then he tipped her chin, so she looked him in the eye.

"Cher, repeat after me. I am beautiful and sexy as hell."

Her eyes got wide, and she blushed from her toes to her very red hair.

"Come on, say it."

She took a deep breath and sighed. "I am beautiful and sexy."

"Oh, now, you didn't say it quite right. I am beautiful and sexy as hell. Try again." He was very serious about this.

She lowered her gaze to his chest and mumbled, "I am beautiful and sexy as hell."

"That will do for now, but we are going to work on your opinion of yourself. Now, turn around and let me get your back."

Cade: Le Beau Brothers

Obeying, she turned toward the spray. He reached around her to rinse her off. His large, strong hands cupped her aching breasts as he pressed his throbbing manhood into the cleft of her backside. He rolled her hardened nipples between his thumbs and forefingers as she moaned in pleasure and pressed herself back into him. Cade took all her weight easily as she laid her head against his shoulder. He tried to stop thrusting between her cheeks, failing epically. Before he completely lost all control, he took the soap again and washed her back. Beginning at her shoulders, he slowly slid his hands down her slick body cupping her buttocks for a moment. Then his hands slid around her hips and between her legs.

Cade growled in need as he stroked the lips protecting her womanhood, gently parting them. Even though they were drenched from the shower, he felt her saturated with need. Sliding his finger through the warm, weeping channel, he elicited a soft cry from Anna. He teased her nub until she was squirming and pressing against his hard, straining manhood. Slowly he slid one finger in, gliding out again, then up and around her nub to return and plunge back in. Her hips started thrusting in time with his fingers. He repeated his ministrations as he added a second finger, filling her. Anna's moans and cries increased as he quickened his pace. Her breathing became ragged, and he held her tighter as she pressed her hands against the sides of the shower for leverage. Then she threw her head back and cried out with a mind–blowing orgasm. If he hadn't been holding her, she would have hit the floor. He slowed his thrusting and held her tightly to him until her body ceased quivering.

As she turned in his arms, she had an astonished expression on her face.

"What?"

"That's never happened before," she breathed. "At least not in real life."

He was confused for a second.

What hasn't happened before?

A man in her shower?

Getting off in the shower?

HOLY COW!!! His eyes got huge.

"You've never had an orgasm before?"

Her whole body blushed with his realization. She just shook her head.

"What the hell has that idiot of an ex–husband been doing all these years!" He didn't know if he should be angry at how she had never had her needs met or rejoice in knowing he had given her the first orgasm of her life. "Well, my beautiful, beguiling mate, that is just the first of a lifetime of orgasms, you have my word." He gave her the charming, lopsided grin he knew she adored.

She giggled at his playfulness, which was exactly what he'd been going for. He never wanted her to feel uncomfortable in his presence.

Sliding her still wet, slippery hands up his abdomen and over his chest, she wrapped her arms around his neck. "Thank you," she whispered.

He was enchanted by his mate. There was no other word for it. He kissed her senseless, and when he felt her shiver, he grabbed a towel to dry her thoroughly from head to toe.

Cade: Le Beau Brothers

A man could get used to this, he thought, as he made sure to dry every inch of her before he took her to bed. The day had been long, and they needed sleep.

Chapter 7

The Big Day!

Cade was experiencing total bliss waking with his mate in his bed. If he had a tail as a human, he would be wagging it. His wolf was rumbling contentedly, making the growl–like noise that was the closest thing a wolf had to purring. His wolf was rolling over on his back wanting his mate to rub his belly and cuddle.

As Anna woke, she stretched like a cat and rolled over. "Good morning," she said through a still sleepy smile.

He grinned at her. "Good morning, gorgeous," he said pulling her in for a proper good–morning kiss. He loved the feel of her soft curves pressed against his body. Wanting more he pulled her in tighter.

He had been disappointed when she put a nightgown on last night. He would have to convince her to sleep in the all–together the first chance he had. He and his wolf didn't care for barriers between them and their mate.

She must have come completely awake as he deepened the kiss, because he felt her fingers thread their way through his hair. He really liked how passionate she got when she played with his hair.

He was ready to make love to her when he felt her pushing him away and pressing him down onto the bed. By the devious expression she wore, he knew she had naughty thoughts running around her pretty little head. He had a feeling he was never going to survive this! Pulling his hands away from her body, he let her explore at her leisure. He was curious to see what she had in mind.

She wanted him on his back with full access to his chest and other parts of his anatomy. She hadn't been allowed to touch, pet, or stroke last night, and dang if she wasn't going to get her some now.

She propped herself up on one arm and began exploring his chest. Softly she skimmed her palm across his pecks, causing his nipples to harden and a rumble to echo around the room.

He tried to reach out and pull her on top of him, but she pressed her palm flat against his chest, shaking her head at him with a mischievous grin.

"No touching, babe. This is my time now."

She rubbed her thumb across his engorged nipple and then rolled it between her thumb and forefinger gently. He closed his eyes and groaned, his breathing becoming heavy.

With a feather–light touch, she skimmed her fingers down his six–pack dipping into every valley as she grazed over them. The effect was like her fingers were riding a mini–rollercoaster. Cade's eyes started to glow and his breathing came faster. Never before, had her touch aroused a man to such a fever pitch.

Moving her hand lower, she felt his happy trail leading her exactly where she wanted to go. She let her fingers glide along the downy soft hair until she felt the tip of his rock hard erection. He was weeping already in preparation for her.

She slid her fingertips partway down his shaft, just enough to wrap around him, below the bulbous head. Holding his gaze, she rubbed the pre–cum across the head of his erection with her thumb. He let out a gasp as she stroked her fist to the base and back again. The action sent him into a growling frenzy, arching off the mattress, pressing himself harder into her hand.

He couldn't help himself as he mindlessly pumped his hips. He wasn't sure if he was in heaven or hell, but, damn, her hands felt amazing. He was nearing his limit when there was a loud banging on the hotel room door.

The sudden loud noise made Anna jump and pull her hands away from him.

He spat out a string of expletives that would make a hard–core biker blush as he jumped out of bed and jammed his legs into a pair of jogging pants. The tenting action left nothing to the imagination.

He smelled Stefan in the hall. No doubt about it, his brother needed killing for this interruption. He heard him chuckling on the other side of the door. That boy had a death wish.

He jerked the door open glaring daggers at Stefan. "You had better have a damn good reason for being here." His lips curled back as his wolf came into his eyes.

Stefan leaned casually with his shoulder against the doorjamb and laid his head against the frame. Cade could tell he was pretending to be cute and innocent knowing it would piss him off even more. Stefan batted his eyelashes at him for good measure. He must really have a death wish.

"I've been waiting patiently. I didn't have the chance to meet your mate the other night. I want to meet her," Stefan said

Cade was not fooled. Stefan knew if he came here today that the odds were very good he would be interrupting something private between him and Anna, and the possibility just egged him on all the more to do it.

"And you had to meet her at the crack of dawn, did you?"

"Well, yeah, I had to come to town for a meeting anyway, so I stopped by for coffee with my new sister–in–law."

He glared and snorted at his brother. He knew exactly what his brother was doing. He was here to cock block him. To Stefan, that was hilarious. Too bad, payback's a bitch.

Both men turned toward the bedroom door almost on cue. "Cade, who's at the door?"

"My soon–to–be–deceased little brother." Cade glared at him again.

Stefan cocked his head and openly glanced over Cade's jogging pants with its glorious display. His grin got even wider.

Cade grabbed him around the neck so fast Stefan didn't have time to react. He hadn't administered a nuggie to his younger brother in a lot of years, but he was getting one today. They were both laughing so hard they couldn't breathe.

Anna walked into the room wearing her bathrobe to find them gasping for air like a couple of fish out of water. She shook her head and mumbled something which sounded like, "Men are all nuts," as she went for the coffee pot.

Stefan cleared his throat to get her attention, earning him another glare from Cade. "Hello, little sister. I'm Stefan, Cade's favorite brother."

Cade let out a snort and joined Anna for a cup of coffee. Picking up his cup, he put his arm around her shoulders to introduce her to his troublesome brother. "Anna, this is my annoying brother, Stefan. He lives to harass me. He was at your apartment with me the night Tim broke in. You may not remember him."

"Oh, but Cade, you make teasing so easy. It's almost not even a challenge." Stefan grinned and winked at Anna. He busted out laughing as Cade snarled at him over his winking at his mate.

"I do recognize you, but we weren't introduced. It's nice to meet you. Thank you for being there."

"I'm grateful I was able to help. It's such a pleasure to meet you."

Anna found Stefan rather amusing and quite the charmer. This man was a heartbreaker all the way. He knew all of Cade's jealousy triggers and had no compunctions about pushing them. She smiled to herself, imagining Cade and Stefan as boys getting into all kinds of trouble. They must have had their share of tussles and black eyes.

Her brothers had teased her growing up, but a brother harassing a brother is different than one teasing a sister.

Even though Stefan poked at Cade to get a rise out of him, she saw the strong bond between them. They might be picking on each other now, but if anyone outside the family threatens one of them in any way, a thunderstorm of trouble would rain down on the fool.

An unexpected thought popped into her mind.

I wonder what Rose would think of Stefan? Naw, maybe not. She goes for a quieter type of guy. He does have five other brothers, so who knows. Maybe one of them would be her type.

She really wanted to see Rose in a happy relationship.

Sipping their coffee, they sat at the table to plan the day.

"So, Stefan, you have a meeting this morning?"

"Yeah, at the new restaurant you offered on. I'm meeting with inspectors and the fire chief to go over your requirements. I meet them in about twenty–five minutes and will probably be with them for close to two hours."

"Email me later and give me a report on whether you think the restaurant will meet my stipulations."

"You got it. Oh, and don't forget, we have a meeting with the committee downstairs at four this afternoon."

"Don't worry, little brother, I'll be there." He picked up Anna's hand brushing his thumb across the velvety skin. "I won't like it, but I'll be there."

Stefan shook his head. "You know you do have to come up for air once in a while."

Cade grinned. "Just wait until you find your mate, and I manufacture all kinds of reasons to pull you away." His eyes twinkled with amusement thinking about the payback Stefan would be receiving.

Stefan stood to go. "Well, you two have a fun day. Try to actually leave the room." He walked around the table to Anna's chair and leaned down quickly giving her a peck on the cheek.

Cade literally exploded out of his chair. The flimsy piece of furniture never stood a chance. He lunged for Stefan's throat just as Stefan dodged right and made a dash for the door laughing like a maniac.

Yep, Stefan's fate was sealed. He was going to die.

Anna reached out and laid her hand on Cade's arm, feeling him shake with his fury. She continued to surprise him with her instinctive reactions. Somehow she knew to not say anything, but just touch him and wait.

Slowly his heart rate calmed and his breathing returned to normal. He touched his forehead to hers. "I'm sorry, cher. I reacted out of instinct. Did I frighten you?"

"I'm all right. It just startled me when the chair went flying. But I get it, really, I do. Plus Stefan was poking you like a bear in a cage ever since he banged on the door. It was just a matter of time before he pushed you too far."

He stared at her, baffled.

She laughed at his expression. "I grew up in a house full of men and spent just over twenty years as the only female in the house. I know how men behave."

"I can't get over how well you take all this craziness I've thrown into your life."

She busted out laughing. "You really are an easy mark for him. He knows just what buttons to push to make you lose it." She shook her head still chuckling. "You seem to forget, we have five years of experiences in our visions. I know what kind of man you are and how protective you can be."

"Yeah, I guess you do. There were one or two occasions in the visions where my protective side reared its head." He looked a little sheepish.

"So what do you have planned for the rest of the day?" she asked.

"Actually, if you'd like to get out of here for a while, it's what do 'we' have planned for the day. Would you like to do a little browsing in the shops and play tourist in the Quarter with me?"

She considered his offer for a minute. "Shopping isn't one of my favorite things. Going to the French Market was one thing, I needed a belt, but window–shopping is just plain painful. I guess I'm one of those rare women who only goes into a store when I need something and I know right where to get it."

Ugh, window–shopping without a set plan of attack, just shoot me now.

She sighed and gave in to please him. "Sure, I guess. Will we be shopping long?"

He seemed confused. Obviously he thought all women lived to shop. "No, I don't think so. Maybe a few shops, and then we can play tourist for the afternoon."

In a few minutes they were out the door of the hotel. Two blocks toward the lake was Royal Street, and a few blocks over on Royal was Cade's final destination.

Cade felt bad he hadn't taught Anna how to shield her thoughts yet, but, damn, she was funny when she thought no one could hear her. He promised himself to teach her soon.

Maybe tomorrow.

Or next week.

He planned to purposely take her in and out of several shops to camouflage his real reason for the shopping trip. He was on a mission, and the secrecy required stealth and cunning.

First, they wandered through a French antiques shop. Poor Anna, she was trying so hard to look interested in the beautiful lamps and furniture. He would try to not torture her too badly. When he felt they had spent enough time in the shop to serve his purpose, he feigned not being able to find anything he wanted to buy so they could continue on.

Next, he chose an art gallery. They had some very interesting art, and when Cade was ready to leave, she almost wanted to stay a little and linger. Almost.

He purposely mixed up the kinds of stores they went into so when he hit the one he actually needed, she wouldn't suspect anything. He noticed a vintage sports shop and almost rubbed his hands together with delight. This was getting fun.

Anna let out a groan as he pulled her toward the sports shop. "Cade, I think it's best you find out now. I'm not into sports. Combine that with shopping and you can just shoot me now."

Cade put on his best pleading puppy–dog face. "Is it okay if we go in for just a minute?"

He could tell she was gritting her teeth and she wore a fake smile that looked more like a grimace. He waited for her answer, interested in what she would say. He didn't really care if they went in; it was just part of the camouflage for his target a block down.

"Okay, I can take it for a few minutes, but you are going to owe me, buster."

"Thanks, cher, it won't take more than a couple minutes."

He made a show of scanning the vintage baseball cards as his excuse for going into the store. If she knew he hadn't actually needed to go in the store she might kill him. He sensed she was almost to her limit by the look on her face and the amount of sighing he heard.

I better get moving before she calls it quits.

"I don't see anything I want. Let's go a little further down the block before we do something else," Cade said.

She gave him a real smile this time and took his hand as they left the store. "So, is there anything specific you are shopping for? I could help if I knew what to look for."

"No, nothing specific. I just wanted to spend the day wandering around the Quarter with my lady." He gave her what he considered his best smile.

She rolled her eyes at him and they both laughed.

Up ahead was his reason for all the effort–the most exclusive jewelry shop in the Quarter. Nothing but the best for his Anna. Jack Sutton Jewelry at 315 Royal Street would have exactly what he wanted.

He tightened his grip slightly on her hand and steered her toward the entrance.

She hissed. "What are you doing?" she demanded as she glared at him.

He looked over his shoulder and shrugged innocently. "What? They have really nice stuff, and my friend, Jack, owns the place. So I thought we might say

"Hi" and enjoy his shop."

Anna growled and mumbled under her breath, "Jewelry shops are worse than sports shops. The man is going to kill me."

That was when he realized, she never wore jewelry in their dreams or in real life. Apparently she wasn't a jewelry girl either.

Cade was already scanning the cases for the perfect item. Not just any piece would do. The ring had to be special and unique, like Anna, or it wouldn't do her justice.

The shop owner walked up. "Hello, Cade, how are you doing?"

"Great, Jack." His glance went to Anna before he looked the owner in the eye, conveying a wealth of information in that pointed stare. She didn't seem to be paying any attention to them, which was good. If she stayed far enough away, he could do this without getting caught.

"I'm looking for a very special gift," Cade whispered and winked.

Jack discreetly winked back. "How much do you want to spend?"

Playing it casual so he wouldn't tip her off to a transaction going down, he shrugged. "Money is no object."

"Okay. Then I have some exquisite, one–of–a–kind pieces over here." Cade followed him to a high–security case at the end of the counter, and immediately saw the ideal ring that would be perfect for his mate. He casually indicated the ring while sliding his black American Express card to Jack concealed under his palm. Before she came into view,

Cade: Le Beau Brothers

Jack quickly slipped the card into his pocket.

Cade moved to a less expensive case to throw her off, pretending to be seriously shopping. "Anna, can you look at these for me?"

Anna was slowly wandering around the shop, and when she heard him call her name she headed back in his direction.

"Which is your favorite?" he asked.

She scanned the case and shrugged. "They are all nice, I guess."

He wasted a few more minutes randomly looking at things to give Jack time to finish the super–secret sale and slip the card and ring to Cade without being seen.

"I guess there isn't anything we want here." He sighed for effect. "Thanks, Jack, I'll see you around."

Chapter 8

The Big Question

Once on the sidewalk, Anna reached out and brushed her fingers against his cheek.

He turned his face into her palm and nuzzled it, then kissed the very center. Smiling, he said, "We have some time before I have to meet Stefan. Would you like to take a carriage ride through the Quarter?"

"I would love to. I've always enjoyed those rides, and the tour guides are interesting to listen to."

"Good." He leaned down and kissed her. With his arm around her shoulders, they strolled to Jackson Square to hire a carriage. The drivers waiting for a fair were lined up along Decatur where water troughs were available to the mules.

He led her to an available carriage, and like the gentleman he was, helped her up. Anna scooted over to make room for him to join her while he paid the driver. For some reason, he had a private conversation with him that Anna couldn't hear. The glances the driver cast at her during the secret tête–à–tête made her a little suspicious.

Cade: Le Beau Brothers

Cade casually hopped into the carriage and acted like he was completely innocent of whatever he was up to. He started pointing out things around them to cover whatever it was he was doing.

He is really bad at being inconspicuous and nonchalant, she mused.

She looked at him skeptically while he did his best to snuggle her against his chest. The driver played it cool, being a perfect cohort in crime and pretended nothing was going on.

The mule pulled them out onto the street, and they started through the Quarter.

The driver turned halfway in his seat. "Let me introduce myself. I'm George, and I'll be your driver today. Are you two visiting our fair city?" he asked.

They looked at each other and both shook their heads.

"Have you taken a ride before?"

"I have several times," said Anna. "I never get tired of the stories you guides have to tell."

"I have as well," Cade added.

George gave her a smile. With a nod he turned and faced forward, which perplexed her. Normally the driver sits sideways in the seat so they can drive and talk to the passengers at the same time.

What are these two up to?

She suppressed a little smile. She wasn't going to make it easy on him by asking what was happening. Instead she closed her eyes, snuggled closer and inhaled the warm, wonderful scent of Cade. For extra measure, she thought about all the hot, steamy things she would do to his body. In explicit detail. Loudly.

She giggled as she heard his heart pounding

rapidly beneath her ear. They rode past a variety of venues throughout the French Quarter. As they passed bars, music drifted out of the open doors. Every kind of music was available in New Orleans, the blues, zydeco, jazz. You name it, they had it.

Cade rested his cheek on the top of her head while he caressed her face, brushing his thumb back and forth across her cheekbone.

Her skin is so soft.

He was gathering his courage to offer her the ring.

Taking a deep breath, he tipped her chin up with his index finger so she would be looking him directly in the eye. He almost couldn't breathe as he held her gaze and gathered his nerve.

He'd planned to wait until tonight. In his mind, they would go to a fancy restaurant with a white linen tablecloth and a candlelight dinner. He'd get down on one knee and, with her tiny hand in his, look deeply into her eyes and ask her to wear his ring. He wanted it to be very romantic, but he honestly couldn't wait any longer.

He twirled a tendril of her hair around his fingers, and cradled the back of her head while gazing into her eyes.

"Anna." It came out as a croak. He cleared his throat to try again as he reached into his pocket.

"Anna, I want you to know, even if we weren't destined mates, I would want you, desire you, and love you. Regardless of whether you ever choose to mate with me, I want you to know, I still want you–no–need you in my life. I want you to commit completely to me, but only when you are ready. In the meantime, please honor me by wearing my ring as a promise to you that I will always love you. I knew the moment I saw this ring it belonged to you and no one else, as my heart belongs to you and only you."

He held out the ring as an offering to her, but what he really held there between his fingers was his entire heart and soul. He was putting it all on the line. She had the power to either make him the happiest man in the world or shred him and leave him bleeding on the floor. He held his breath and started to sweat.

Anna nodded, tears of joy shining in her eyes. She was so beautiful, her hazel eyes sparkling and blazing green. Cade's hands shook as he slid the ring onto her finger. It was perfect. He took a shaky breath and kissed her like he had never kissed a woman before. Tears of joy rolled down her face giving them both wet cheeks.

He pulled back. "What's wrong? Did I do something wrong. I screwed this up, didn't I."

She shook her head. "No, babe, not at all. No man has ever treated me like this before. Last time I was given a ring, I was informed I was getting married, not asked. I certainly have never received a promise of love with such eloquence."

He kissed her cheeks until all evidence of happy tears were erased. "Gorgeous," he whispered throatily, but he wasn't looking at the ring. His eyes were fixed firmly on her face.

Reaching for her hand, he caressed her skin and played with the ring he had just placed on her finger. It was like silk under his fingertips. He may have billions in the bank, but she was the most precious thing he had now that she had accepted his promise. Compared to her, money meant nothing. He felt he was a completely different person than the man who'd walked into the Crescent City Brewhouse and found this beautiful woman sitting at the bar cursing at her phone.

Anna was speechless. She couldn't believe he had given her his heart completely. She stared at the gorgeous ring. It was the most beautiful ring she'd ever seen in her life. She had no idea how he had known canary diamonds were her favorite, but he had– somehow he had.

The center stone was a huge, bright yellow diamond set into a dainty white gold filigree band and crown. She wasn't sure just how large the center stone was, but she guessed close to three carats. Six smaller, flawless white diamonds ran down each side of the band. The stones were so brilliant, they were blinding. The dainty swirling filigree pattern of the band set off the stones perfectly. No other setting would do these stones justice.

About a block down, the driver pulled to the curb and Cade helped her down. They were in front of Crescent City Brewhouse again, where they had met the very first time, in real life anyway.

Anna smiled broadly at him, and he said, "It all began here, and if it's all right with you, I would like to order a celebratory glass of champagne here to toast to the most beautiful woman in the world accepting my ring."

Anna gave him her biggest smile, took his hand, and walked with him into the Brewhouse.

Richie happened to be working. His face lit up as he saw Anna walking in with Cade. Unbeknownst to the humans that frequented the Brewhouse, Richie was also a shifter. He knew that Cade would make Anna very happy, and that was what he wanted most for his good friend.

Wiping his hands on a bar towel, he walked to the corner nearest Cade and Anna. "Hi guy's. What would you like?"

"Champagne, Richie, and bring the bottle."

"What's the celebration, Cade?" Richie had a pretty good idea but he thought he'd play along and ask anyway.

"This gorgeous lady has agreed to wear my ring. I couldn't be happier. I can't imagine myself without her in my life or what I ever did before she was in it." Cade was looking into her eyes like a lovesick puppy.

Anna sat quietly watching the exchange between the two friends. Her heart thumped wildly. She couldn't believe how happy she was. It was amazing how life could take a turn.

*****

It was 3:30 in the afternoon when they returned to the hotel after a joyous celebration with friends at the Brewhouse. That meant he had only thirty minutes to get to the meeting downstairs with Stefan and the lawyers. It was killing him to even think about leaving Anna's side. With the mating not completed, his wolf was nervous and pacing. For a shifter who had found his mate but hadn't completed the ritual, it was downright uncomfortable to be any amount of distance apart.

Her room was on the twenty–sixth floor, and the meeting was in a boardroom on the third floor.

Twenty–three floors apart. He hoped since they would be in the same building, the discomfort wouldn't be too bad. Not like being miles apart; still he wanted this meeting to be short, like fifteen minutes short. Then again, maybe she would come along to the meeting?

"Cher, would you like to join me downstairs?" He hoped her answer would be yes, even though he felt a bit selfish wanting her to sit in a meeting with lawyers, completely bored, just to ease his own issues.

She glanced at her laptop. "I was really hoping to spend some time on my new client's project. If being there is important to you I'll go, but, if not, I'd rather get started on their branding."

He actually turned red. This was the first time she had seen him blush. "Of course, you have work to do as well."

Forgive me, mon amour.

Her eyes softened. *Silly wolf, there's nothing to forgive, especially when the request comes from your desire to be with me. I prefer to not be apart as well, but eventually we do need to rejoin the world.*

He brushed his fingers along her cheek before turning to the bedroom to change for the meeting. Minutes later he emerged in a tailored black silk suit, crisp white shirt and royal blue tie. He was HOT! Man, she loved a man in a suit.

She bit her lower lip as she looked him slowly up and down before she finally met his eyes. He let out a low, sexy growl. "Keep looking at me like that and I'll never get to the meeting."

She gave him a saucy grin and chewed on her fingertip as her eyes and her thoughts heated. She was imagining peeling the suit off him slowly as she licked and nibbled the exposed flesh being revealed.

He moved so fast she didn't see him take a step. Suddenly he was right in front of her wrapping his strong arms around her and yanking her into his hard body as he buried his face in her hair.

The suddenness of his reaction knocked the breath right out of her. "Cade!"

"I can't think straight when you fantasize like that! Wicked woman, sending me to a meeting hard as a rock. You did that on purpose. You're killing me here."

She ran her fingertip down his chest provocatively, playfully. "Well, then I guess you'll hurry back as quickly as you can."

He let out a frustrated groan and took possession of her mouth, savoring her for a few seconds before he had to tear himself away. "I expect you naked and in bed when I return." A playful expression spread across his face and a wicked gleam shone in his eyes.

"Oh, I'll be here. I'm just not sure I will be in the bed though." She couldn't help sending him an image of her wet and soapy in the shower.

He gave her a look that promised retaliation when he returned and walked out the door.

*****

Shortly after Cade left to meet Stefan, Anna heard a knock on her door. She thought Cade was back and had forgotten his keycard.

He wasn't.

Tim stood in the doorframe. Before she could slam the door in his face, he blocked it with his foot and pushed his way in.

Taken by surprise, she stumbled back and fell into one of the dining room chairs.

"What are you doing here?" she demanded. "You're not allowed to come near me. Get out!" Her pointed finger jabbed toward the door as she stood again.

Tim shrugged. "I need to talk to you."

"You've got to be kidding me!" Her eyes were blazing and had gone dark. Tim was too stupid to notice. "You are completely insane."

He acted as if he hadn't heard a word she'd said. "Anna, I was wrong. I miss you so much, and I want you back."

She was speechless for a moment. She couldn't believe what this idiot had said. Did

he actually believe she would take him back? *Oh, Hell to the NO!*

He tried to grab her left hand. "Where did you get that ring? Did HE give you that? You slut!"

Anna burst out laughing. She wasn't going to respond to the ring comment. "You don't want me back. The only reason you're here now is because you've seen me with another man. A very handsome man. And you can't stand the idea I'm with someone other than you. Cade's good looks and amazing body make you look like a container of leftover food left to rot at the back of the refrigerator, growing slimy and covered in ugly mold. Not only is he major eye candy, but he's a wonderful man, something you'll never be." She leaned closer to Tim and wrinkled her nose. "You even smell like rotten food. Show a modicum of pride and shower once in a while."

Cade: Le Beau Brothers

Anna's laughing at him triggered something in Tim. He clenched his fists and turned a unique shade of red. In a haze of rage, he stumbled to the door and flipped the security lock.

Anna started to panic. She was locked in and he looked completely crazed.

He turned to her with a sneer on his face. "You need to learn a lesson, Anna. You are mine. You will always be mine. It looks like I have to remind you of that."

She frantically searched for a weapon. The only thing within reach was a lamp. Taking a deep breath, she calmed her mind. She had to remain focused and wait for him to be in position.

She watched as he circled the furniture closing in on her. The instant he was within striking distance, she snatched the lamp and smashed him in the head. Tim went down hard.

To get to the door, she'd have to pass him. The bedroom was the only place to go. As she ran for it, he snagged her ankle, tripping her. Anna kicked at his hand, noticing the white cast on his other arm, courtesy of Cade from that night in her apartment. The hate in his eyes sent fear skittering to her core. She scrambled on her hands and knees the last few feet to the safety of the bedroom.

Sounds came from behind her. No doubt Tim was on his feet. In the bedroom, she reached to lock the door, but before she could enable the lock, it thrust open, knocking her into the room and against the bed.

Tim launched into the room and pinned her with his body to the mattress. His hand wrapped around her throat. She wasn't having any of this. She kneed him as hard as she could then scrambled across the bed into the bathroom.

Panic began to take control, her eyes searching every item looking for a weapon. Hair brush, toothpaste, trashcan, open fingernail kit. BINGO. She snagged the steel nail file.

Tim leaned against the doorframe and chuckled. "Looks like the end of the line, wife."

Sink and counter at her back, anger burned with fear in her stomach. "Ex–wife."

He glanced at the ring on her hand. "I think that little rock right there is the answer to my problems. It cost, what? Fifty thousand?"

Anna whipped her hand behind her. "Touch it and die," she growled. He'd struck a nerve and she instantly went from panic to furious.

He scowled and stepped forward. "I don't like this man. And I won't have him touching you. After I get you home, I think I'll come back and take care of him, too." Tim charged into the room.

Anna gripped the nail file tightly. She wasn't sure she could stab someone, not even Tim, until he'd threatened the man she loved. "I won't let you hurt Cade."

With a snarl, Tim grabbed her by the hair and punched her in the face with his cast. She almost blacked out from the blow. Refusing to go down, she forced her way to consciousness, pulled her arm back as far as she could, and slammed the nail file into his chest.

Tim screamed and released her.

Anna ran for the door to the hall. Before she could get it open he was charging her. She waited until he was a breath away and spun out of reach, sending him crashing into the door. He was momentarily stunned by the impact. Running the few steps to the kitchenette, her eyes swept the space for a weapon. Nothing. Her only choice was to try to make it to the hotel hallway again. She turned for the door.

Without warning, his hands snaked out and wrapped around her neck.

She twisted to the side using her self–defense moves to break free.

Unexpectedly, Cade and Stefan exploded through the door, throwing it open so hard the crash sounded like a sonic boom in the hotel room. The impact of the door created a huge hole in the wall the exact shape of the door handle. It vibrated on its hinges as if quivering in fear. Cade's eyes were blazing green and glowing brightly. His lips were pulled back and his canines were extended. They flashed dangerously as he roared and snarled in a red haze of rage. Stefan grabbed Cade in a crushing bear hug, using all his strength to stop him from ripping the stupid human to shreds.

Anna wasn't going to give Tim the chance to carry out his threat against her mate. So while Tim stood staring at Cade's partial upper body shift, she pulled her fist back and smashed Tim in the jaw with a right hook. With one punch she sent him to the floor, out cold.

She shook her hand trying to ease the sting from the blow she'd dealt Tim; as she turned to see Cade and Stefan no longer struggling by the door. They both went completely still for a moment, in shock at the sight of Anna punching Tim's lights out.

As his shock wore off, Cade broke free from

Stefan. He snatched Tim off the floor by the arm and threw him across the room. Tim's limp form smashed into the wall and slid to the floor. Before Stefan could stop him, Cade's wolf took over, slamming Tim onto the table and hammering his head onto the wooden surface several times.

Stefan leapt into action. "Cade, you need to stop. You can't kill him, not here." Stefan had Cade in a bear hug again. It was taking all he had to hold his brother back.

Anna came out of her own shock. "Cade?"

Hearing his mate's voice triggered something in his mind. He gathered his control and Stefan released him to attend to his mate.

He opened his arms wide as she leapt into them. Anna buried her face in his chest and started to shake as the emotions of what had just happened flooded her. Cade carried her to the couch and held her, whispering reassurances to her.

A storm of men ran down the hall, as the police appeared on the scene. One of the neighbors must have called 9–1–1 when they heard the battle raging.

Still shaking with fury, Cade glanced at the nearest officer. "Get that piece of shit out of my sight before I rip him apart."

Stefan spoke quietly in the hall with another officer, giving his statement. Cade and Anna needed time alone.

Once the scene cleared and Anna was safe, Cade spoke with the officers. He made sure they had everything they needed for their report. The last thing he wanted was her at the police station facing another nightmare.

Cade: Le Beau Brothers

Cade and Anna ignored the officers as they left. They just held each other for comfort. He slid his hands under her shirt and rubbed small circles slowly all across her back, needing to sooth her and also calm his wolf by touching her, skin to skin. Needing more contact with his mate, he rubbed his chin across the top of her head. Gently, he took her right hand, the one she had punched Tim with, and kissed each knuckle leaving no skin untouched. Then he kissed her cheek where she had been punched. "I will get ice for that, mon amour."

He stroked a lock of hair from her face. "Are you okay? Are you hurt anywhere else?"

"I'm fine. A little shaken, but not hurt. I'm tougher than I look."

"I almost killed him when I saw his hands on you. If Stefan hadn't been here, I would have been calling my lawyer to defend me on murder charges," he confessed.

"You did come through that door like an avenging angel. I'm not sure the wall will ever be the same." She grinned. "Sure you went a little wolfy, but in the end you held it together. I'm proud of you and your control. I'm sure other shifters, given the same situation, would have shredded first and hidden the body later."

"You really laid him out, cher," he said grinning.

"I grew up with older brothers, so I learned to throw a punch." She laughed.

Her brows knit together as she thought about what all had happened. "How'd you know to come back to the room?"

"I heard you wondering what Tim was doing here and felt your anger."

"I'm so glad you did, I'm not sure I would have made it out of here alive if you hadn't come back," she said as she snuggled into his lap.

"I will always come for you. I'm so sorry you were hurt at all. I promised to keep you safe and I failed. I promise to be more diligent, but I also think we should look into classes for you. Maybe karate or some other form of defense. As much as I always want to be the one who saves you, you proved today we may need a backup plan."

"I've thought about taking a class like that. And I agree, I think that's a really good idea. And, who knows, I might just learn some new moves to use on you. By the time I'm a black belt I will know all kinds of new 'things.'" She waggled her eyebrows in emphasis.

Chapter 9

Cade's Wolf

Night fell on the city and they still sat together on the couch.

"Do you feel like ordering in or going out?" he asked, nuzzling her neck.

"Room service sounds good to me. I don't feel like going out again tonight."

"All right, I need a shower before we eat. I'll only be a minute, and then I'll call down for dinner," he said as he left the room.

Ten minutes later, he strode into the living room as he called the kitchen on his cell phone, ordering their dinner. Toweling his hair dry, he joined her on the couch.

Sighing, she rested her back against his side.

He loved to power lounge holding her this way. Wrapping an arm around her, he cuddled her close and laid his cheek on the top of her head.

"I meant to tell you, I need to be on a building site tomorrow morning first thing. It'll take me some time to get there, so I may be gone when you wake up. I will be gone all day, but I would like to have a fun night on the town when I get back. Does that work for you?" Cade asked.

"I have a busy day tomorrow as well. A fun night sounds wonderful."

He smiled into her hair. Without warning, he sent her the feeling of love and contentment, and then waited for her reaction.

She was grinning and her eyes were shining bright as she twisted in his arms. "Was that you?"

He tried to feign innocence but didn't pull it off at all. They both laughed.

"I wanted to show you a few more things you'll be able to do as my mate. Sending feelings as well as words is one of them."

Anna's grin widened. "That's so cool! All the things shifters can do are so cool, and being able to do them, too, is going to be fun. What else will I be able to do?"

He sent her a picture of the way he saw her when they were snuggling on the bed and she had been sleeping peacefully the other night. In his eyes, she was the most beautiful woman he had ever seen. He wanted her to see herself the way he saw her.

She gasped as the image appeared in her mind. Cade watched her search his eyes and saw a hint of disbelief in her gaze. She obviously still had doubts about her attraction for him.

Is that truly the way you see me? You can't really see me like I'm some great beauty.

Yes, mon amour, that is exactly the way I see you. You are the most beautiful and sexy woman I have ever seen. Your softness and curves drive me wild.

She snuggled into his arms, grinning like the Cheshire Cat.

You do realize I think you are the hottest, sexiest man I have ever seen. When I dreamed about you, I thought I'd made you up. You were so perfect, there was no way you could be real.

"Hey, I have been wondering about something. How were we able to dream about each other when we'd never met? I don't understand how that was possible."

Cade rubbed his cheek against her hair. "I have heard rumors that when a shifter or his mate has particularly strong magic, they can experience visions like ours. I inherited the powers of the gypsies and voodoo through my mother. The additional magic in our family is why we are so strong among the shifters. Perhaps our connection is extra strong and our souls were reaching out for each other."

He sent her the feeling of his fingers caressing the side of her face.

First she jumped slightly and then she squealed with delight. She twisted out of his arms so she was facing him again. "You so have to teach me how to do that!"

He busted out laughing. What a delight she was to him. Teaching her their ways and their magic was going to be such a pleasure.

"I'll give you lessons after we've eaten dinner. I hear the waiter coming down the hall."

Her mouth literally dropped open. "You can actually hear something like a person coming down the hall? Will I be able to hear like that, too?"

Chuckling, he nodded. "Yes, you will."

The waiter set their dinner on the dining table, lit a romantic candle and poured glasses of wine before he excused himself.

Cade held her chair and then went around the table to his own seat. Lifting his glass for a toast, he gave her the sweetest smile she had ever seen as he tapped his wine glass with hers. "Here's to new beginnings, my beautiful woman, and the blessings of fate."

They both sipped their wine and enjoyed a scrumptious meal prepared to Cade's specific orders. The hotel restaurant had all the foods he enjoyed most, charbroiled oysters, seafood gumbo, seared scallops, and a mouth–watering steak with sour cream smashed bliss potatoes. He looked forward to sharing them with her. This was a feast!

Carefully, he scooped gumbo from his bowl, offering the spoonful of steaming deliciousness to her. "I want to feed my mate."

Without hesitation, she grinned, and then wrapped her lips around the spoon.

Anna picked up her fork and knife.

This might be fun, she thought.

Choosing the scallops, she cut off a bite and offered the morsel to him. His face lit up like a Christmas tree as he accepted the tasty bite.

Next he cut steak to feed her. She leaned forward and accepted the perfectly medium rare bite.

Taking advantage of the moment he decided to approach the subject of mating with her. "Cher, I love taking care of you and providing all of your wants and needs. I would love nothing more than to do so for the rest of our lives." He gazed at her with a very serious

Cade: Le Beau Brothers

expression bordering on apprehension. "I hope someday you'll agree to complete the mating ritual with me. But I'll never pressure you. The choice is yours. When you're ready."

No more was said about the mating ritual as they enjoyed the rest of the meal.

She had never been treated like this by anyone. They continued to feed each other until the meal was finished.

"Would you like dessert?" Cade asked in his deeply hypnotic voice.

A glorious cheesecake and a four–layer chocolate cake sat on the wet bar across the room. She looked over at the choices and groaned, "I can't eat another bite right now."

Nodding his agreement, he came around to her chair and helped her rise.

Placing his hand on her lower back, he steered them to the couch, sharing the rest of the wine from dinner while watching television.

Cade was languidly lying with his head in her lap, rumbling from her touch.

Suddenly, she realized she was stroking his hair like you would pet a dog. She pulled her hand back, hoping she hadn't insulted him in any way.

"Don't stop, bébé. I love to be touched and stroked. Shifters may seem human, but we have a lot of wolf in us, too, and the wolf craves touch." That gave him an idea. "Would you like to see my wolf? You only saw a leg yesterday. Would you like to actually meet the animal?"

She practically squealed with delight. "Can I? Is he like the wolf in my dreams?"

He stood and surveyed the room. For what he had in mind, the bedroom would work best, so he took her hand. After he seated her on the edge of the bed, he stepped back a couple paces. Then in a heartbeat, where he had stood, was now a one–hundred–sixty pound black and silver wolf.

Holy mackerel! You're HUGE!

Walking toward her slowly, he wagged his tail so he wouldn't scare her. When he was close enough to touch her, he set his head on the bed next to her leg, allowing her to initiate contact.

Cher, you can pet me, I won't bite.

"Geez! You could've warned me you could still talk to me as a wolf. Dang, you scared about five years off my life."

His wolf chuffed a laugh at her reaction. Laughing, she stroked his head and scratched his ears. Her touch pleased his wolf and he rumbled his pleasure.

She had grown up with large dogs, and she loved to pet them and give them back scratches, especially between the back hips where dogs can't reach to get that one itch which drives them crazy.

She scratched his neck, then all down his back, giving him special attention between his hipbones. He was in wolf heaven. He honestly didn't think it could get any better. Then she slid off the bed to sit on the floor with him and gave his wolf a full body hug. He was wrong. It got better. Hands down, he adored this woman, plain and simple.

He waited until she was in just the right position and shifted back to human. He had her on his lap in a flash, right there on the floor. "You never cease to amaze me. I can't wait to meet your wolf."

"I'll be able to shift and everything, too?"

"Oh, yeah. It's all part of the magic in the ritual. You'll receive magical powers like I have and a wolf guardian. I bet you have a sexy russet colored wolf that is sassy as hell."

"Speaking of color, I noticed your wolf is the same color as the highlights in your hair. Is that a coincidence?"

"No, all shifters have hair which contains the color of their wolf mixed in."

"What are all the magical powers shifters have?"

"There are several generally known powers. Shifting into a wolf and possessing the ability to dress or undress with a thought, instantaneously. In the shifter community, we jokingly refer to it as 'poofing'. We also heal ten times faster than humans, and we can move so rapidly that the human eye can't detect us. You already know mates can talk telepathically and send caresses and feelings of emotion through the use of magic.

"Plus, each shifter is born with one additional gift. That ability manifests during childhood." Cade suddenly found a speck of lint on the carpet very interesting.

"What's your additional gift?" she asked.

"I don't usually talk about it. It's kind of embarrassing." He poked at the lint again.

"I'd like to know, if you're willing to tell me."

He blushed a bright red. "My gift is a genius level of intelligence."

"What can you do with that?" she asked.

"I can solve any puzzle or code. I naturally see a

pattern emerge if there is one. That's why I analyze all the family investments."

"Why don't you like to talk about it? I think your gift is really cool."

"It sounds arrogant to say you're a genius," he said as he raised his gaze from the floor.

"Okay. Let's think of a new name for your gift then. We could simply call it code breaker," she said smiling. "The next time someone asks, tell them you're a code breaker."

"I like it. I'll do that." He smiled again. Anna could do that for him, she was able to see a problem and solve it easily, without drama.

She cocked her head. Her expression telegraphed she was thinking about something.

"Does it hurt when you change?" she asked.

"Not at all. You think the change and allow it to happen. It's instantaneous. One minute you're human and the next you have the body and senses of a wolf, but you're still in control of your thoughts and body at all times."

Cade realized now would be a good time to teach her how to shield her thoughts. "I should give you a lesson in building walls in your mind. If you guard your thoughts, I'll only hear what you direct at me and nothing else. I love your thoughts, but I don't want to invade your privacy."

"Okay. What do I do?"

"It's fairly simple. Picture a wall surrounding your mind. Any wall, stone, brick, you decide, and see it rise up as a protection so strong it can't be breached."

Cade: Le Beau Brothers

She closed her eyes and pictured a solid brick wall. "I think I have it."

"Now, think something really loudly, but don't direct it at me."

Anna sang loudly in her mind.

"Did you think something?"

Excitedly, she clapped her hands. "I did it!"

*****

It was 9:00 p.m. when Cade's phone rang. She quickly learned Cade was a pacer when he spoke on the phone. Some people are incapable of sitting still during a call, and apparently he fell into that category. The caller was his mother inviting them to a family barbeque so they could meet Anna. She was a little nervous to meet his family, but, from the conversation, she knew meeting his parents was important to him.

Ending the call, he stopped in front of her with his hand extended. She took it without question, curious to see what he had in mind.

"We haven't finished our date."

She frowned. "Date?"

"Our private dinner," he said grinning. "There is one thing that would make this night complete. Dessert." His eyes shone with heat.

"You're right. It's still on the bar," she said teasing him.

It was obvious to her that he had ideas other than eating cheesecake with a fork. She made to step toward the bar when she was brought up short by his arms snaking around her. She squealed and laughed as he trapped her to his body.

"I have a different dessert in mind. And I'm planning on savoring every lick and nibble."

Her eyes shone with excitement turning very green and her heart began to race. The way he devoured her with his stare–it was intense. The stark desire in his eyes made her stomach flutter. His eyes slowly lowered and left a trail of heat in their wake. The look was possessing. Passionate. Hungry.

Her entire body burned with heat that pooled low making her achy and needy. She couldn't remember the last time just looking at a man made her this hot.

As if her hands had a mind of their own, they reached for him. Her fingers splayed wide across his chest, moving intuitively over him. Anna played with the buttons on his shirt as she considered removing the offending material to get to his bare skin. She just wanted to rub herself all over him, skin to skin.

Crushing her to him, he backed her toward the bedroom, devouring her lips. His tongue plundered her mouth with stark need. "Anna," he breathed her name like a plea. "I'll try to be as gentle as possible."

Their bond had slowly grown over the last five years without them even knowing. Now that they were together, the mating bond was becoming stronger by the minute. She wanted him with an urgency she had never felt before.

She wrapped her arms around his neck and, without a thought, lifted her legs and wrapped them tightly around his waist. He was hers and she was not ashamed to enjoy their sexuality. She had never had this feeling of freedom to enjoy herself without the taboos people put on sex. Anna had grown up in a very religious family, and then had been belittled by men for her weight all her life. She felt none of that with this man.

Her hands roamed freely, memorizing every inch of him as intimately as he was memorizing every curve and valley of her. She was rapidly losing control as the passion continued to burn hotter.

Cade growled his approval and quickened his pace to the bed. She clung to him while he had one arm around her waist and one hand tangled in her hair. He urged her head back with gentle pressure, so he could lick and nibble her neck. "I love your scent."

Both Cade, the man, and his wolf, needed to make love to their mate. Having sex wouldn't complete the ritual, but it would be enough until she was able to give herself to them completely.

He lowered her to the bed, his body following. Having magic to undress became his favorite gift. Removing their clothing by human means was too slow for him at this moment. "Mon dieu. You have a beautiful body."

His chest rumbled as he brought his mouth back to hers before blazing a trail of kisses across her jaw and down her neck, pausing to nuzzle where his bite would be.

Anna moaned as he fueled her desire with each caress. She laced her fingers through his hair, rubbing the silky strands between her fingers. Cade sensed the intensity of her desire burning higher with each caress he gave as she arched into his seeking hands. They were both breathing heavily as he slowly nibbled and stroked every inch of her body.

"I love your mouth on me."

Worshipping her, he slowly ran his palms to her

hips and up her stomach to her ribs. Dipping his head, he traced each rib with his tongue as he made his way to her aching breasts.

She skimmed her fingers down his chest as he worked his way toward her nipples. As he drew closer, her fingertips skimmed his erection and she felt it jump. The contact caused him to suck in a breath. As if in fascination, she traced the length of him with her fingertips before wrapping her fist around him. He thought his head was going to explode in ecstasy simply from her caress.

"Cher, your touch feels so good, but you need to stop or this will be over before we begin. I have thought of nothing but making love to you in the flesh for five years. I want to make this incredible for you, but I need all the control I can muster to hold out."

Anna gave him a pretty pout as she released him.

He felt hunger flare in his eyes, making them glow hotter, as he lowered his head to continue the trail he was blazing to her nipples, the hard buds strained for his attention. Cade slowly laved her left nipple while he teased the right with his thumb and forefinger. Circling the taut peak one last time with his tongue, he took her into his mouth, suckling deeply. His wonderful torture had her arching, encouraging him to take more. Cade rumbled low in his chest in total ecstasy and bliss. Releasing the left breast he switched his attention to the right and repeated the ministrations, not wanting to leave a spot of her lovely skin untouched.

With one last pull on her breast, he kissed his way to her hips. Cade gently nipped and laved her hipbone, as he ran his palm up her thigh, drawing a gasp from

Cade: Le Beau Brothers

Anna as he reached her dripping core. Stroking her inner thigh, he gave her one long, slow lick. He felt her body clench as her hips moved in time to his attentions. He took his time enjoying her unique taste. His tongue plunged deeply, bringing Anna almost off the bed as her body arched closer to his mouth wanting more.

He heard her whispering his name over and over like a prayer. He wanted her screaming his name. To add further pleasure, Cade sucked her nub as he inserted one finger. He stole a glance at her face, and caught her biting her lip as if trying not to scream. "Let go for me, cher. Scream if you want to."

He felt her fingers entwined in his hair as she moaned, her head thrashing back and forth. He pushed her climax higher and higher. Adding a second finger, he stretched her further while his thumb worked its magic on her nub. His thrusting fingers moved in and out before circling her clit in a rhythm pushing her over the edge. Cade sensed she was close, her hips were bucking wildly trying to take him deeper and harder. Suddenly her channel clamped down on him as she came hard, screaming in ecstasy.

"That's it, mon amour, cum for me."

Gradually the quaking of her body eased to fine tremors. She was so beautiful with that sultry look on her face. He loved the way she responded to him. Cade's wolf howled in satisfaction at its mate's climax.

He continued to slowly lap at her until the pulsing and tremors subsided. Then he kissed his way back up to her lips, settling himself in the cradle of her hips. He captured her gaze with a sweltering look, as he licked his fingers clean. He was painfully aroused and he needed relief as he rubbed his thick, hot shaft through the slick lips of her opening.

He was a large man in more than one aspect, and as hard as a rock, engorged with need. Maintaining eye contact, he slowly entered her. Only an inch or two in, breathing hard, he stopped, to allow her to adjust to his size. As Anna relaxed for him, he slid in a little further. He had to grit his teeth to gain control as he stopped again. "Are you okay?"

Anna was literally whimpering, "More, Cade, I need more."

He drew back slightly and thrust in to the hilt, starting a slow rhythm that drove her crazy. With each deep stroke her moans became louder.

She wrapped her arms around him and clung to his shoulders, digging her nails in as her orgasm started to build again. She had never experienced pleasure like she did with this man.

He increased the tempo of his thrusting as he felt her channel tightening on him in a mind–blowing chokehold. "Mon dieu! You're so tight." His teeth clenched as he fought to let her climax first.

A few more deep strokes had her back arching as she clamped down on him screaming out her orgasm. Unable to hold out any longer, as she came, he joined her in his own release.

Cade carefully rolled to the side. He didn't want to crush her with his weight. They both lay panting, trying to recover. Reaching out, he tucked her against his side with her head on his shoulder. Once he was able to move again, he gave her the sweetest kiss she had ever been given. Gazing at her, he saw love reflected back at him in her eyes.

Cade: Le Beau Brothers

Cade gathered the bedding to cover them and cradled her in his arms as she fell asleep. His wolf was howling a love song; he was so content to have his mate right where he wanted her. Life was going to be fantastic with this woman by his side. To him, she was sheer perfection. He fell asleep with his nose buried in her hair and a sappy grin on his face.

Chapter 10

Fun on Bourbon St.

She heard the electronic room key trip the lock as he came back from his busy day.

Dropping his briefcase on the floor, he swept her into his arms. "I missed you like crazy today," he said, rubbing his chin in her hair.

Laughing, she answered, "I missed you, too. Did everything go well at the site?"

"Perfectly. Construction will be completed a month ahead of schedule. Let's get changed and enjoy our night on the town before you have to meet my family tomorrow," he chuckled.

"Why do you laugh when you say that?" Given that he'd laughed, Anna wasn't sure if she should be nervous about meeting them.

"I have an interesting but loving family. You will see for yourself at the barbeque. Don't worry; I'm sure they'll adore you. Stefan already does."

She decided to take his word for it and not worry. "What would you like to do tonight? I need to know what to wear."

Cade got a wicked glint in his eye, and she just

shook her head at him and started searching through her clothes.

"I was thinking we could have a little fun on Bourbon Street, walk around and see what we find to do. People watching there is almost as good as Jackson Square."

"All right, jeans it is." Anna grabbed her favorite pair of Lee comfort–stretch jeans and a pretty silk blouse. The fabric was the perfect shade of blue to really enhance her hair color and make her skin glow. She brushed out her hair and freshened her face. She hated makeup, and only applied mascara on a daily basis. Cade liked her that way, he once told her; a woman was more beautiful as natural as possible.

They were in the Quarter in no time, walking hand in hand. The crowds tended to start building after 7:00 p.m., and it was still early. They decided to take a table on the balcony of one of the restaurants on Bourbon and people–watch for a while as they sipped Hurricanes.

"About the family party, my house is on part of the family estate. When we go to the barbeque, would you like to see it?"

"I'd love to see your house. This is the first time I've heard you even mention having one."

"I wanted to move you straight there after the whole Tim thing, but I didn't think you were ready, so I didn't say anything."

"I'd love to see where you live. By the way, what should I wear for this barbecue? Are jeans and a T–shirt okay, or should I be dressier?" She really wanted to make a good first impression.

"Jeans are good, that's what I'm wearing. Just so

you know, a couple of my brothers will be there. Three of them are away right now, but Stefan, Marcus, and Simon are home."

"Will there be any other women?" The party sounded like it was going to be all men with no women to chat with. She really wanted to get some tips on this whole mate thing and being a shifter.

"Well, my mother will be there, but so far I'm the only one of us brothers who has found his mate. Sorry, cher. If you want, I could have my mother invite some of the local female shifters."

"No, I think meeting your brothers and parents will be enough." She so didn't want to meet a bunch of random people tomorrow.

Cade was busy watching a silver painted mime performing directly below their table. This was the perfect opportunity for Anna to test their link and see if he would feel her touch him. She closed her eyes and concentrated on visualizing her hand sliding slowly down his stomach and creeping across the front of his jeans.

He let out a hiss, and his head jerked up in shocked surprise. Anna burst out laughing at his reaction. "I guess it really does work," she said as innocently as possible.

His eyes smoldered, and suddenly Anna felt his large hands cupping her breasts. She let out a gasp and crossed her arms over her chest as if the barrier would help. He barked out a laugh of amusement. "Don't start what you can't finish, mon coeur."

Anna tilted her head. "What does 'mon coeur' mean? You aren't calling me names, are you?" She knew he wouldn't, but she had to tease him a little.

Cade: Le Beau Brothers

He shook his head. "Never!" and held his hands over his heart dramatically. "Mon coeur is 'my heart' in French. Being a New Orleans native, I grew up speaking a bit of the old language."

That made her smile. "Mon coeur. I like it."

*****

He took her hand in his. "Then I shall call you my heart more often." He raised her knuckles and kissed them gently.

Anna concentrated again and visualized stroking his face with her fingertips. He slowly raised his eyes from her hand. "You're getting the hang of sending touch very quickly. I knew you would."

He looked thoughtful for a moment. "Try sending me an emotion."

Anna considered that. What emotion should she try? She decided the easiest would be love. Not really having any idea how to send something as abstract as an emotion, she tried to simply project love to him. The fullness of her heart, the feeling of butterflies in her stomach every time she gazed at him.

His smile grew huge. "I felt that, cher." He leaned forward like he was going to whisper a secret to her. "You love me." Then he winked and sat back again.

Anna swatted at him playfully. Yes, she did love him. In the time they had been together, including their vision time, she had fallen madly in love with him. She had never felt anything like this before.

She knew people would whisper and talk about her accepting his ring so quickly, but this was not a normal relationship in any shape or form. For one, he wasn't human, and, two, the whole mate, two–halves–of–a–soul thing caused the people involved to instantly want and need to be together.

Being mates is nothing like humans falling in love slowly over time as they get to know one another, she thought. *It seems mates have an instant attraction and strong sexual need to be together all the time, at least from what I'm experiencing. I swear I can feel my heart and soul crying out for Cade's. This need is so intense and deeply emotional. From what he says, the getting–to–know–your–mate part often comes second.*

As she was thinking this through, something occurred to her. Was this normal for every mated pair? "Babe, have there ever been mates who, after they mated and got to know each other, found they really didn't like the other person? What if they mated and after a few months hated each other?"

He smiled at her concerned expression. "No, cher, I've never heard of that ever happening. The two people are a perfect match in every way and encompass all the aspects the other person wants and desires in a perfect life partner."

She exhaled a sigh with the breath she didn't realize she had been holding. "I'm relieved to hear that. Because, the way I already feel about you, I won't be able to hold out much longer."

He cocked a lopsided grin. "You don't have to wait at all. I'll be right here, ready to oblige you the moment you decide to complete the ritual."

She concentrated on her hands in her lap.

Why am I waiting anyway? Is it society's pressures or my own doubts?

Cade: Le Beau Brothers

She was pretty sure she was once again bowing to what the reactions would be from friends and family. They would say she was moving on too quickly. They had no idea she had actually been with him for five years.

But honestly, why on Earth should others' opinions even matter to me?

In that instant, she realized she'd made up her mind.

A mating ritual was a private matter between the two of them and not recognized by human laws as a marriage, anyway. The ritual was stronger and deeper than a marriage ceremony. There were no laws governing a mating, or legal marriage license requirements. Now she'd have to guard her thoughts so later, when they were in the hotel room, she could surprise him with the one thing he wanted most.

Cade sat quietly sipping his drink, watching the emotions flow across Anna's expressive face.

He could spend hours quietly watching her and not get bored. He swore he could hear the wheels turning as she worked out whatever was going on in that beautiful head. She wore the expression of deep thought as her teeth worried her lower lip. In the blink of an eye, her face relaxed into a small smile of satisfaction. Whatever she had decided, she was pleased with it. He glanced away to the street performer before she caught him studying her.

They sat for about an hour longer people–watching and enjoying Hurricanes before he suggested they stroll the street below and pick a place for dinner. He paid the bill and they headed out for the rest of the night.

Reaching for her hand, he threaded his fingers with hers as they walked and discussed dinner options.

Cade caught her thoughts as they made their way down the street. Anna had noticed all the women they passed would turn to watch him go by. He honestly didn't care about any other woman but his mate. He smiled as she realized he only had eyes for her, no one else existed to him. She really liked the fact he didn't check out every set of breasts that walked by.

He was so proud of her when she held her head a little higher. She was finally beginning to see herself the way he saw her. Chuckling as they continued down the street, he gave her hand a little squeeze.

On the sidewalk, two bars ahead, he saw a man he knew, one he had hoped to see here tonight. They walked over to him and he made the introductions. "Etienne, this is my Anna. Anna, this is my longtime friend, Etienne."

She extended her hand to shake his. He took it, and while holding it, respectfully gave her a slight bow. "I am honored to meet Cade's beautiful mate."

"It's very nice to meet you as well."

How does this man know I'm your mate?

I'll explain in a minute.

"Etienne, I may have need of your unique services in the next few days if you'll be available."

"Cade, as always, I am at your service. Simply tell me when, where, and who."

Anna was seriously intrigued now. Who the heck was this guy and what were they talking about?

Cade said his goodbyes, and they continued down the street. Anna decided to wait until they were seated for dinner to find out what that was all about.

Cade: Le Beau Brothers

They spotted a restaurant with a cozy patio and made their way toward it to check out their menu posted on the exterior wall. "What do you think, mon coeur? Does anything look good to you?"

"Sure does." She wasn't looking at the menu.

He growled. "What did I tell you about starting something you can't finish. Now, behave yourself," he said playfully.

Slowly she gave him one more once over and turned her eyes to the menu. "The barbeque shrimp sounds fabulous."

That was enough to satisfy him; decision made. As they stepped through the main door, a hostess greeted them instantly as if she was dying for something to do. It was still fairly early and the dinner crowd hadn't started to fill the restaurant yet. "Two for dinner?" she asked.

"Yes, and a patio table, please," he said. As they walked to the table he whispered in her ear, "I preferred to eat outdoors whenever possible. My wolf is more comfortable in open spaces."

They were promptly seated and settled in for a bit more people–watching while they waited for their food. Across the street, a couple doors down, was a gentleman's club. The bouncers and two of the barely covered young ladies were on the sidewalk working the few pedestrians milling around.

Glasses of water showed up on the table, bringing their attention back to the server.

"Would you like to hear the specials?" she asked as she snapped her gum.

Cade scowled at her slightly in disapproval. "No, thank you. Please bring the crab cakes to start. Then, the barbeque shrimp dinner and the grilled red snapper with red beans and collard greens. We'll also take a bottle of the German Riesling, as well." He handed her the menus and turned his attention back to Anna.

"I'm sorry, cher, I didn't realize the wait staff here was so poorly trained." He was honestly horrified.

She giggled at his pinched expression. "It's all right. You eat at restaurants that aren't stuffy five–star snob collectors sometimes, don't you?"

He blustered a little for show. "Of course I do. I just wanted tonight to be perfect."

"One waitress with a nervous gum habit won't ruin our night," she chided him.

"Very true," he agreed. "I just enjoy playing and bantering with my mate."

"Now perhaps you can clue me in on who Etienne is and what you were talking about." She leaned forward with her arm on the table tucking her hand under her chin for effect. She wasn't letting this go without answers.

"Etienne is a vampire." Cade waited for that bomb to echo around a bit.

"You've got to be kidding me. Next you will tell me fairies are real, too."

He tipped his head and cocked an eyebrow as if to say, "Well, um, yeah, they are."

"Oh good, Lord, how do people not know this?" She was talking to herself more than to him.

"We have rules and consequences in place to keep all the paranormals secret from humans."

She had a thoughtful expression while sipping her water.

Cade: Le Beau Brothers

Okay, Anna, you're a big girl. You can handle this. Now, suck it up and quit being a sissy.

He snorted water out his nose at her little rah–rah speech to herself.

"Oh, shut up." She laughed at him. "So how did he know I am your mate?"

Wiping the water from his face, "Well, I'd like to discuss that with you." He paused and reached for her hand. This was going to be a difficult conversation, it already had his wolf in a frenzy just thinking about it.

"I've had endless worry and concern about Tim. I've received numerous reports of him bragging about how he is going to force you to come crawling back to him. Because of my extensive holdings throughout the French Quarter and New Orleans in general, there's little I don't know the minute it happens." He waited to see if Anna would ask any questions. When she continued to wait quietly, he began again.

"I'm sorry to tell you, Tim has gotten himself in deep with the local crime syndicate. These people are very dangerous, and I can't have you anywhere on their radar. I'm sure you don't want your sons near the situation either." He waited again.

Anna took a deep breath and sighed. "I always knew he was a complete idiot, but this is more than even I imagined. What are you going to ask the vampire to do?" She wasn't sure she wanted to know, but, like a car pileup on the interstate, she couldn't look away.

"Vampires can make humans forget things and also plant ideas into their heads. He can make Tim want to leave you alone. He can also get Tim to keep his illegal dealings away from your boys."

Anna sat nodding as she thought that through. She didn't want him anywhere near her or the boys.

"Etienne will look him in the eye and tell him what to do. He'll also take a small amount of his blood so he can track Tim if need be and read his mind at any time to verify he is following his commands. That's it."

"Do it," was all she said. End of conversation, and she preferred to never speak of it again.

He took her cue and dropped the subject.

The food was incredible, and dessert was a decadent triple chocolate bread pudding that, when paired with Drambuie and coffee, was orgasmic. They chatted, people–watched, and fed each other the warm, chocolate slice of heaven. All too soon, dinner was finished. The two hours they'd been eating and playing had flown by.

During dinner Cade had come up with a plan to woo his incredible mate. His destination was about two blocks from where they sat. "I want to talk to Etienne, and then let's walk further down the street and check out the clubs and music. Maybe there is a good band playing," he offered as a cover for his actual plans.

It didn't take long to locate Etienne on the street. "I have a man that I'd like to have modified," Cade told him.

Etienne nodded his head once in acceptance. "Email the particulars and consider it done."

Cade thanked him and they said their goodbyes.

Chapter 11

The fun continues

They strolled slower due to the heavy meal they had just enjoyed. Anna couldn't remember the last time she had eaten that much, but, dang, the dinner and dessert were too good to stop. Leaving chocolate dessert unfinished should be considered a crime anyway. It was just not done.

A stripper tried to entice them into a gentleman's club, quietly offering Cade a threesome as she checked out Anna with a hungry look. He politely declined, thanked her and they continued down the sidewalk.

They reached the corner of Bourbon Street and St. Peters Street, the home of the Cat's Meow karaoke bar. He gently guided her through the crowd as they dodged the masses of people constantly moving up and down the ten blocks of world famous asphalt.

The open walls of the bar allowed the public on the sidewalk and street to peer in from almost any angle. They could see the stage in the corner with the DJ playing the selected music of the karaoke singers. That's when she saw Stefan sitting at a table close to the stage with another man who appeared he could be related to both Cade and Stefan. Cade turned to her with a raised eyebrow, and tipped his head toward the bar. "Looks like it could be entertaining. Let's check it out."

They worked their way to the front of the room to Stefan's table. The men rose like old world gentlemen as she approached. Cade put his hand on her lower back and began the introductions. "Anna, this is my brother, Marcus. Marcus, this is my beautiful Anna."

She graciously reached to shake Marcus's hand. With a twinkle in his eye instead of shaking it, he lifted it to his lips.

Cade showed his brother his teeth with a very dangerous growl.

Both Stefan and Marcus guffawed loudly as they laughed until they had tears in their eyes.

They settled in for the combination of star quality accountants living their alternative lives and drunken college girls screaming into the microphone. To her surprise, Cade walked over to the DJ, and it looked like he signed up to sing. Then he whispered to the man while slipping him something. She would swear he was passing the guy money for some reason.

The latest suit–wearing businessman finished his rendition of House of the Rising Son by the Animals from 1964. To Anna's surprise, the DJ signaled to Cade and handed him the microphone. So that was what he was paying for, he wanted the next spot in line to sing. Who knew he sang karaoke? She prepared herself to hold her face in a positive expression in case he really stunk up the joint.

Stefan and Marcus wore identical grins. Their reactions had her interest piqued.

Cade: Le Beau Brothers

What did these two know that I don't? Maybe he's a closet rock star.

"This is for Anna, the love of my life."

A few heartbeats passed and the music started. It only took three notes to play and she recognized the song– "The Power of Love" by Huey Lewis & the News. She covered her mouth in shock and astonishment. Tapping her foot in time to the music, her smile was so huge that her face started to hurt a little, but she couldn't stop. No one had ever sung to her before.

The microphone was cordless, allowing Cade to walk over to the table and really work it. "Tougher than diamonds, rich like cream, stronger and harder than a bad girl's dream," he sang as he played with her new ring. He brushed his fingers along the back of her shoulders and stepped in front of her chair.

Oh, my gosh. You're incredible!

Cade had the perfect growly voice and sounded so much like Huey Lewis.

He poured his heart and soul into this song for her, telling her in every word how he felt about her. His gaze was filled with love and longing shone in his eyes as he sang the chorus, "That's the power of love, that's the power of love."

Stefan and Marcus were eating this up like candy.

She could tell he was ignoring them and focusing on her. Not wanting to miss one second of his performance, her eyes were riveted to him as he danced away from her showing off moves she had no idea he had. He was a complete showman and the crowd loved him. Cade did a slow, sexy dance back to her, seducing her with every searing look and word he sang. He finished the song on one knee in front of her while holding her hand. She had never been so blown away with love for anyone. If she had harbored any doubts about mating with him before walking through the bar doors, they were shattered now.

Anna had tears of love and joy streaming down her face. Her heart was so full it felt like it would burst right out of her chest.

Without looking, Cade handed the microphone to the DJ behind him and took her face in both of his hands. She received the sweetest, most passion–filled kiss ever.

Stefan cleared his throat. "Come on guys, get a room."

Cade slowly released her lips, gave her one last soft kiss on her lower lip, and snarled at his brother for the interruption.

Anna wiped the remaining tears from her face and shyly excused herself from the table to freshen up in the ladies' room. She was sure she looked hideous after all the happy tears and running mascara.

Weaving through the crowd to get to the far corner of the room where the bathrooms were located was a challenge to say the least. She had to go around the far edge of the long oak bar lined with partiers. She had almost gotten to the door when a man grabbed her arm. It was obvious by the way he swayed he had imbibed a few too many of whatever he was drinking.

The man leaned in with his alcohol–laced breath and whispered in her ear so no one else would hear. Not that they could, over the volume of the bar. "You are a mate and yet unclaimed."

Cade: Le Beau Brothers

She pulled back from him trying to free her arm, but he had a tight grip on her and wasn't about to let go. "What do you mean?" She was confused as to how he knew she was Cade's mate.

"You bear the mark of a highly desired mate. Rare and prized. I will be your mate and care for you."

She was stunned by both his mention of some mark and declaration he would be her mate.

What the heck is he talking about?

In a flash of snarling, teeth, and partially shifted wolf, the man was ripped from her and thrown to the floor. Cade would have torn him to shreds in front of a bar full of humans if Stefan and Marcus hadn't been there to pull him off.

*****

As the man went down still clutching her arm, Anna was knocked to the floor. He lost his grip on her as Cade barreled into him, and she did her best to scramble away from the struggling men.

Stefan and Marcus signaled to the dozen other shifters scattered around the bar to create a visual shield around Cade and Anna. A wolf in the middle of a bar on Bourbon Street would definitely make the news. Pictures and videos would be posted within minutes if the scene was not blocked from the public eye. Anna almost screamed when another stranger pushed through the wall of shifters and grabbed the idiot from the floor, yanking him to his feet. Teeth were snapping and animalistic snarls and growls were coming from both men.

V.A. Dold

"You stupid whelp," the older man said. "You never lay hands on another man's mate. EVER!" He backhanded the younger man so hard his head snapped back at a very painful angle.

She winced and shrank further back.

Cade held onto his wolf by a thread; it threatened to burst out needing to protect its fallen mate.

He was reduced to a wild, rabid animal at the sight of his mate frightened and huddled on the floor. The beast who dared touch her would die a gruesome, painful death.

The brothers stepped between the two men and Anna providing a safety net for Cade to tend to his mate and collect himself. If that idiot had half a brain, he would stay very quiet and not draw any more attention to himself.

Cade's hands shook so badly, he was afraid to touch her for fear of frightening her more. Crouching down, he reached for her. But stopped, his hands hovered over her body shaking frantically with mind–numbing fear.

Oh, God! Please don't be afraid of me, Anna.

Babe? Why would I ever be afraid of you?

Anna, oh, baby, I'm so sorry. I saw him grab your arm and whisper in your ear and I just lost my control.

I'm okay, but can I get off this disgusting floor?

He let out the breath he had been holding, stood and scooped her off the floor into his arms. He stood for a minute with his eyes closed, breathing her in and calming his wolf.

"Baby? Cade, are you okay? You're shaking."

"Yes, mon précieux mate. I just need to recover from seeing you fall to the ground possibly injured."

143

Cade: Le Beau Brothers

"Can you put me down? It's a little embarrassing to be carried around in public."

"Give me another minute with you in my arms. I need to feel you are safe. Just let me touch you, okay?"

She wrapped her arms around his neck and allowed him what he needed. After what seemed like fifteen minutes, he slowly lowered her feet to the floor, sliding her body along his, keeping his arms wrapped around her to keep her close. He wasn't able to release her completely yet.

When he finally had control, he swept Anna behind him and confronted the whelp who was being held by the scruff of his neck by a man who must be a father figure to him. He was in human form, and yet it sure looked like the man had him by the scruff of the neck like a dog.

"How dare you touch my mate," Cade growled dangerously.

The elder stood tall and proud, but didn't look Cade directly in the eye. "Pardon me, my Lord. Do you wish to claim blood rights or the judgment against Travis?"

Cade shot a worried glance at Anna out of the corner of his eye. He didn't want to explain the man's strange way of addressing him or expose her to that barbarian form of justice. It was his right, but he wouldn't exercise it for Anna's sake. "No, I leave his punishment to you. You will teach him some manners and the rules of mate etiquette. The next wolf he offends may not let him off so easily. Now, may I ask your name?"

He bowed low once for Cade and for each of his brothers, "I am Jason Ledet."

"Jason, I hold you responsible for his actions. Don't let it be heard that he has acted so inappropriately again. I won't let him off a second time." Cade forced Jason to look him directly in the eye, then the elder lowered his eyes in submission again.

Cade turned his attention back to Anna.

Anna leaned in and whispered, "Babe, could we please leave and go back to the hotel? I need a little air."

He gave her a single nod and created a path through the crowd by the sheer menace radiating from him.

They turned down St. Peter Street in order to grab a cab back to the hotel. The distance was a far walk from the bar, and they were both overly stressed. A ride back would help to ease their nerves.

He helped Anna into the car, and then slid in next to her, pulling her close. He had to touch her or he would lose his grip on his wolf right there in the back seat. There was silence between them all the way back to her room. She was in deep thought and he didn't want to remind her of what had just happened.

Afraid if he made too much noise he would break the spell, he closed the hotel room door quietly behind them. His mate was back to the safety of her room and his wolf could relax. He sat silently as long as he was able. "Cher? Are you all right? You are so quiet it's terrifying me," he spoke, barely above a whisper.

She snuggled into him like a puppy burrowed into a pile of blankets. "I'm fine. But I have questions about what happened and what was said, and I'm just not sure how to ask them."

"What was said that you're wondering about?" He gently stroked her hair and waited for whatever was coming. He would answer her openly and honestly. There were no lies between mates.

"The man from the bar, Travis, said I have some kind of mark. Something about rare mates. What's he talking about?"

"The perfect circle birthmark on your shoulder is the mark of a very rare and powerful female shifter."

She sat up straight searching his face. "But it's just a regular birthmark, and prior to meeting you I wasn't even close to being a shifter."

"Shifters don't normally bear many female children. Case in point, I have all brothers. Most of our mates are human women who are converted during the mating. Throughout history females bearing your birthmark became extremely powerful shifters. A male is naturally at his most powerful at the full moon. But a female with your mark is crazy powerful at the new moon. The mark is a dark circle to symbolize the phase of the lunar cycle when the moon is completely dark."

"So I'm some kind of super powerful shifter?" She shook her head as if subconsciously she were denying the possibility.

"Yes, actually you are. Your power is another reason why we were able to connect in the visions. I wasn't the only one bringing us together. You were helping to create the link as well," he said proudly.

"He also said he knew I wasn't claimed and he'd be my mate."

For another wolf to say such a thing set his wolf into a snarling frenzy. He didn't realize he was snarling viciously out loud until he saw Anna stand and step away from him.

He instantly stopped. Shit, he did it again. He had to stop scaring his own mate. "I'm sorry, mon amour. I still have limited control after what happened in the bar. Please forgive my grouchy wolf and sit with me again."

Hesitantly she sat. She was a little stiff when he tried to pull her back in, so he let her have her space. "What's claiming blood rights and Royal judgment?"

He hung his head. He really didn't want to tell her about the horrors of blood rights, or expose her to the knowledge of such practices so soon after the scene at the bar. "I'd rather not talk about that right now. It's brutal and ugly. I don't agree with the punishment, and only the most archaic pack families still practice it. Can we please talk about it another time?"

She nodded. "Can I ask you something really personal about you and not insult you?"

He got a quizzical expression. "Um, sure."

"Will you always be so crazy about another man touching me?"

He chuckled to himself. "Yes and no. I'll always be sensitive and protective, but until we complete the mating, I'll be a lot worse. I'm sorry, cher, my instinctive reactions are something I really can't control very well."

"Why did Jason call you 'my Lord' and bow like he did?"

He groaned and scrubbed his hands through his hair. "My family is the royal line of the shifters. My father is their king and we sons are considered princes. My family is the direct descendants of the original shifters that were created."

She searched his face, then averted her eyes and sighed strangely.

He tucked a finger under her chin and raised her eyes to his. "What is it, my love?"

"There's no way I can measure up to be part of a royal family. You should have told me before."

"This reaction is why I didn't tell you. We don't rule like you imagine a royal family would. People look up to us because of our bloodlines. The family has not held court of any kind since before I was born."

She scooted over and snuggled back in to his chest. Having her close was perfect as far as he was concerned.

Anna reviewed everything they had spoken about the last few days. Cade said there is only one mate for a shifter, that her soul is the other half of his, and yet he wasn't rushing her to accept him. He was letting her get to know him with no pressure to make a choice. As a matter of fact, he hadn't even mentioned mating since he gave her the ring unless she brought it up or asked a question.

Cade might seem and act human most of the time, but he wasn't human, and it occurred to her that she placed him being a shifter and not human into the plus column. Recalling her time with Tim, she really had no desire to ever be with another human man. And hadn't she invented Cade in her mind, or at least thought she had, shifter and all, and been blissfully happy?

Well, here he was in her life, in the flesh. Did she really have a reason to hesitate? Was there a reason to wait? She suddenly realized there wasn't. Sure, tonight was scary, but it had also been amazing. Being together, the song he sang just for her. Up until the other shifter made a move on her, he'd been perfect. The night had been perfect.

He would never try to change her. Plus, he adored her curvy figure. He actually didn't want her to be skinny.

In that moment as she sat quietly, she realized she could never see herself without him. She loved him. She wanted and needed him. She'd already made up her mind on the balcony over Bourbon Street. There was no reason to change her decision.

After what felt like a lifetime, Anna raised her head, looked him in the eyes, and said with all the resolve she had, "Let's do this."

Chapter 12

I accept you …

"What are you saying? I need to hear you say the words." His eyes bounced back and forth desperately searching her face for the answer. He was almost afraid to believe he'd heard her correctly.

She brushed his hair from his face as she looked at him with her incredible, expressive eyes. She had captured his heart with her gaze and he never wanted to be released.

"I've thought my decision through."

"Completely?"

"In Detail."

She reached up and gently cupped his face. "I love you. Except for my children, I don't think I'd ever known real unconditional love until I met you."

She leaned in and kissed him gently. "I'm ready to be your mate," she whispered in his ear.

He was thrilled and terrified all at the same time. "Are you sure?"

"Absolutely."

Immediately, he scooped her up and almost ran to the bed. He was going to have to make sure to slow

150

down. He was so excited he was afraid he would rush through the ritual. He wanted this to be perfect for her.

This was the moment he'd dreamed of for over one hundred and fifty years, ever since he had become a mature shifter. He was like a teenager about to have sex for the first time, all nerves and thumbs. Gone were all his smooth moves and confidence.

He set her on the edge of the mattress, sank down to the floor and laid his head in her lap. He was so thankful for this woman, and her accepting him as her mate overwhelmed him more than he'd expected. He hadn't been prepared for this reaction to her acceptance.

Anna intuitively knew to give him a minute to compose himself and remained silent, stroking his hair. When a minute passed and he hadn't moved, she wondered if perhaps his wolf was still struggling with the stress of the night.

"Cade? Baby? Please look at me." She gently lifted his face to gaze into his eyes.

"Would it help if you let your wolf out for a few minutes?" She could tell his hesitancy was more than just mating jitters.

"Are you sure? You've been through so much today."

"I suggested it, didn't I? Let him out so I can pet him."

He stood and stepped back. A heartbeat later he was the beautiful, very large, black and silver wolf. He whined and laid down where he stood.

Come on, babe, move closer to me.

The wolf's head lifted off its paws and his ears twitched forward. Instead of standing to walk to the

151

Cade: Le Beau Brothers

bed, he crawled on his belly to her feet and gave her a lick.

She squealed and pulled her foot up. "Eww, feet are gross."

He chuffed at her and let his tongue hang out of the side of his mouth.

She giggled and slid off the bed to join him on the floor. Cade rolled to his side and she snuggled up behind him, pressing herself against his back and stroking him. He closed his eyes and his chest rumbled contentedly.

Embracing him on the floor, she rubbed her face in his fur and asked. "Are you feeling better now?"

Without answering he shifted to human right in her arms, conveniently forgetting to put his clothes back on. He rolled over to face her with a twinkle in his eyes. "Have I told you lately you're amazing?"

"I'm not sure you have yet today," she teased. "Better get on that, slacker."

He wrapped his arms around her and gave her the lightest kiss on her forehead. "You never cease to amaze me. You always know what I need and provide it without a thought."

"Don't all mates provide for each other?"

"Yes, but not always so generously. You give wholeheartedly, whatever it takes to supply what I need."

"That's not a hardship. I want to do it."

"Exactly. Come on, let's take this important night to the bed." He helped her up and reached for the buttons on the blouse she wore. "I'd like to admire my mate." He slowly unbuttoned the shirt one button at a time revealing her creamy skin inch by inch.

152

Cade released the final button and eased the silky fabric off her shoulders. Her blouse slid down her arms and floated to the floor, pooling at her feet. With a growl of appreciation, he tucked his thumbs under her bra straps and eased them off her shoulders, then reached around her to pop the eyehooks so her glorious breasts would be released to him.

She lowered her arms to allow it to fall to the floor as he slid his hands along her collarbones and up her neck to cup her face. His chest rumbled as he brought his lips to hers, pausing for a moment, enveloping himself in her scent. He kissed her gently, easing her lips apart and searching with his tongue in an unhurried exploration. Their tongues reached for each other, dancing and caressing. With a little popping sound, he released her lower lip.

Then, his palms trailed down her ribcage and over her soft, round belly to stop at the button of her jeans. With the flick of his wrist, the button was opened and its zipper inched down. He ran his hands around her hips inside her jeans, then pushed them along with her panties down her legs to the floor so she could step out of them. His chest rumbled as he brought his mouth back to hers; he wanted to devour her.

Never interrupting his kiss, he tucked one arm behind her knees and swung her into his arms. He laid her on the bed before covering her with his body. Slowly he burned a trail of kisses across her jaw and down her neck, stopping to give special attention to the spot, which would bear his bite. Cade traced her collarbone with his tongue and burned another trail to her breast. He gave her left nipple a flick with his tongue.

Cade: Le Beau Brothers

"Cade," she gasped arching her back and grasping his hair in clinched fists. She needed more contact with his delicious torturing tongue. He chuckled and licked her again more slowly, curling his tongue around the engorged peak. She moaned, on the verge of begging. He would have none of that. Filling his hot, hungry mouth with her breast, he suckled her deeply–strong pulls that made her stomach clench and heat pool low between her thighs. At the same time, he rolled her right nipple with the perfect amount of pressure to heighten her pleasure, yet not cause pain.

Giving her left breast one last slow lick, he moved to the right, fully intending to give her right breast an equal amount of attention. He was nothing if not thorough, and tonight was the most important night of his and Anna's lives. He wanted her to remember this night and the way he made love to her for the rest of her life. He was fueling her desire with each caress, each lick, driving her arousal higher.

She laced her fingers through his fabulous hair rubbing the silky strands between her fingers. She arched into his seeking mouth, the ecstasy was indescribable as the intensity of her desire burned higher. Anna's head thrashed side to side as she moaned. He was going to make her orgasm with just his mouth.

He felt she was close. He wasn't ready for her to turn into a contented puddle of goo.

He released her right breast and kissed his way back to her lips. They were both breathing and trembling with need. Slowing things down, he caressed and stroked every inch of her body. He wanted to memorize every curve. "I adore your body, cher."

"I'm rather fond of yours, too," she panted. Anna loosened her fingers from his hair and skimmed them down his back and up to his shoulders. She loved the feel of his skin. As she reached his strong, wide shoulders, she let her fingertips begin a scorching path across his chest. She was memorizing him as much as he was her. Slowly she circled his hard male nipple with her thumb. Cade let out a little hiss as she rolled it between her thumb and finger–she was making his eyes glow green with desire. He was so excited by her attentions, she had to give the hard little peak a lick to see what he would do. His eyes burned even brighter as he growled in approval.

I guess you like that, wolf man.

She purposely sent him the thought, which made him growl louder.

She brushed his nipple one last time with her thumb before letting her fingertips slowly glide over the ripples and valleys of his abdomen. His muscles quivered and clenched under her light touch, fanning the flames of his arousal. The pads of her fingers skimmed his erection, and she felt the hard length of him jump as he sucked in his breath. With every caress, his erection twitched, bouncing in her light hold. She traced the length of him with her fingers before wrapping her fist around him.

Oh, God, Anna, cher, you're killing me. We have to be careful, I can't cum yet.

A wicked gleam sparked in her eye as her lips followed the same trail her fingertips had taken. She wanted to taste all of his luscious skin.

Cade didn't know if he was going to be able to last as her lips and tongue deliciously tortured his

Cade: Le Beau Brothers

shoulders and then down his chest. She took his nipple into her hot seeking mouth and suckled. Then she laved him with her tongue before nibbling and licking each curve and valley of his abdomen. He was barely holding it together, but he wanted to give her this freedom to explore his body. He clutched the bed sheet in his hands as he tried to think of anything that would assist him in holding his release. He needed to save his finish for the ritual.

Cute, fluffy bunnies.

That got his wolf salivating for a hunt.

Shit, not good.

Stefan's hairy ass. UGH!

It worked, but now he'd have that visual burned into his cortex until the end of time.

He yelled when she took him deeply into her mouth. Taking him all the way to the back of her throat and sucking hard.

Shit, cher you gotta stop, mon coeur. I can't take anymore.

She released him and stuck out her lower lip, then kissed her way up his heaving chest. He heard her inhale in his scent before kissing him lightly on the lips. He knew she was trying to look as innocent as she could. Cade just shook his head and chuckled at her acting skills.

He slowly ran his palms to her hips and up her stomach to her ribs, worshipping her body. Before beginning the claiming ritual, he needed to give them both a minute to cool down or they wouldn't last long enough to complete the claiming.

A minute later he asked, "Are you ready, Anna?" He needed to do the ritual before he lost control and

156

ruined the night for them.

"Yes," she said with complete resolve in her voice.

"Will you give yourself, body and soul, to complete this man and his wolf?

"Will you unite your life with mine, bond your future with mine, and merge your half of our soul to mine, and in doing so complete the mating ritual?" He held his breath and waited for her response.

"I will give myself, body and soul, to complete you as a man and his wolf.

"I will unite my life with yours, bond my future to yours, and merge my half of our soul with yours. I will complete the mating ritual with you," she stated her answer in a strong, unwavering voice.

He slowly kissed her, laying hot little kisses down her body to her hip; gently nipping and kissing as he ran his palm up her inner thigh to her weeping core. She gasped when he covered her dripping core with his entire hand. He stroked her back and forth, open palmed, before carefully parting her lips with one finger, circling her hardened nub before sliding it deep inside. He repeated the action over and over. Circle and thrust. Circle and thrust. The arousal Cade fueled was about to push her over the edge.

He kissed his way from her hip to her drenched core. He stroked her hips as he gave her one long, slow lick. Her body clenched and jumped. She arched off the bed toward his mouth, begging him with her body to give her more.

"I love how you taste," he growled then plunged his tongue inside. She screamed; the pleasure was so intense. He lapped at her juices as he inserted one finger into her. She bucked against his finger needing more.

Moaning, her head thrashed back and forth as he pushed her higher and higher, stroking in and out, then two fingers were stretching her while his tongue worked its magic on her nub. He thrust in and out and circled her clit in a tempo that took her breath away. Before she orgasmed, he removed his fingers, and, with one last lick, prowled up her body and cradled his hips between her thighs.

He was painfully aroused, thick and long. He had never been so hard. Slowly, he rubbed his erection through her damp curls preparing to make love to her as his mate. Cade locked eyes with her and slowly entered her. He made sure she had time to adjust to his size, then he slid in a little further. When she was relaxed, he drew back slightly and thrust in to the hilt. Slowly he rocked with small thrusts.

"I claim you as my mate." The magic swirled around them with his first words.

"I belong to you as you belong to me. I give you my heart and my body. I will protect you even with my life. I give you all I am. I share my half of our soul to complete you. I share my magic with you." Cade rocked forward, kissed her lightly on the lips and nuzzled her neck. He lapped at the spot where her shoulder and neck met, once, twice, a third time, and then bit, piercing the flesh with his extremely sharp canines.

Anna cried out as the shock of pain faded to pure bliss.

He swallowed the little bit of blood seeping from the wound he had made, licking gently as he started his gentle thrusting again.

"I beseech the great Luna Goddess to bless you and your wolf guardian.

"You are my mate to cherish today and for all time.

"I claim you as my mate."

It felt as if something had just whooshed into her body, but there was nothing to be seen by the human eye. She felt fuller, more complete than she'd ever felt in her life. For the first time she truly belonged. She knew she wouldn't feel odd or out of place anymore. The piece that had been missing was found.

"Now you need to repeat the words back to me, my love, and bite me back."

Taking a deep breath, she spoke unwaveringly "I claim you as my mate. I belong to you as you belong to me. I give you my heart and my body. I will protect you even with my life. I give you all I am. I share my half of our soul to complete you."

Anna swore she felt their souls come together, as if tiny knitting needles rapidly closed the gap between the two halves to leave a complete, brightly shining soul.

"I share my magic with you." He lowered himself so she could reach his neck. She hesitantly nuzzled him. Not sure what to do, she copied him by lapping at the spot where she would have to bite him. Once, twice, a third time. Suddenly razor sharp canines erupted in her mouth. At first the new teeth startled her; they felt strange behind her lips. She wasn't sure how she would be able to talk with such large teeth in the way. Before she finished the thought, instinct took over, and she bit down piercing his flesh.

Cade: Le Beau Brothers

Cade yelled out as she sank her teeth, and she knew he felt the same erotic experience she had. He bit his lip hard, drawing blood as he strained, seeming to hold himself back, shaking with the effort.

Unexpectedly, he was hit by an invisible force that knocked him backwards. The blow almost caused her to rip his throat with her canines, she both felt and saw the impact.

"What the heck was that?"

She swallowed the little bit of blood that seeped from the wound she'd made, licking gently to stop the bleeding. "I don't know, but I felt it too."

"I beseech the great Luna Goddess to bless you and your wolf guardian.

"You are my mate to cherish today and for all time. I claim you as my mate."

With the ritual words completed, he started a slow, deep thrusting rhythm that drove her crazy, pulling almost completely out before sliding all the way back in to the hilt. With each deep stroke he heard her moan a little louder.

Anna wrapped her arms around him and clung to his shoulders. She would never get enough of this man and the pleasure he gave her.

As she got closer to her climax, he began thrusting in earnest.

"I can't believe you're mine, really mine. Mon dieu! You're so tight, you feel so good."

She encircled her legs tightly around his thrusting hips, locking her ankles behind his sweet ass. She met him thrust for thrust. Suddenly she felt like she was exploding with ecstasy. Her channel clamped down on him as she came hard screaming his name.

V.A. Dold

She had him in a tight–fisting grip, which was the last straw. He joined her in his own release. Fine tremors quaked her body, milking him with rhythmic clenching.

Gasping, he collapsed to her side, not wanting to crush her with his weight. She was so beautiful with a completely sated look on her face, and he was honored to be the one allowed to put it there for the rest of their lives.

"That was incredible," she breathed, reaching up to run her fingers along his jaw.

"Yes, it was," he panted. "We are really mated." It came out as an awe–filled statement.

Anna was breathing heavily, still recovering. "Yes, I do believe we are." She giggled a little. "You are mine, Cade Le Beau. For the next twelve hundred or so years." She smiled a huge smile. "My five–year plan worked, now you're stuck with me." She laughed as she teased him.

"Are you sure you're not the one who was snared in my trap?" he teased back. "The Goddess works in the strangest ways, but I am glad she found a way to bring us together."

His wolf howled in satisfaction and hopped around like a happy pup. He wanted to meet his new wolf mate. Cade had to settle him down. One thing at a time for their mate, shifting to her wolf could wait for another time.

After a few minutes of recovery, he propped himself up on one elbow as he absently caressed his mate.

HIS MATE.

Damn, he liked the sound of that. He just wanted

to lie there and gaze at her in his bed.

"I felt something strange after you said your part of the ritual." She recalled the feeling, not sure what to make of it.

"Can you explain what it felt like?"

"It was as if something whooshed into my body and filled me up like air filling a balloon."

"I would guess that was your wolf being joined to you. It's hard to explain, but it's like having another soul, a wild animal wolf soul, sharing your body."

Anna quietly considered his explanation. "I think you're right, that makes sense. So how long will it be before I can shift?"

He hesitated. "You can shift at any time, but I wouldn't recommend trying right now. Shifting when you are already tired can leave you stuck as a wolf until you have the energy to shift back."

She sure didn't want to spend what was essentially her wedding night as a wolf. Waiting until morning was a more than acceptable option.

"Remember that weird energy hitting me? It almost knocked me off the bed." That was something he'd never heard could happen during the claiming.

"I felt it too. It happened when I said I would offer to share my magic with you. I think you just got amped up." She grinned at him.

"I didn't think of that. You do have a ton of power. I think you're right, I received power from you in return." Cade was awed by that.

Chapter 13

Conversion

Not more than five minutes later Anna didn't feel well. Maybe she had eaten something that made her sick? She placed her hand over her stomach, as the muscles began to cramp a little. Then she felt a sharp twinge that eased a moment later.

The pain was etched on her face. He could see it. He sensed it.

"Do you feel all right? Can I get you anything?" Cade's brows were tight with worry.

"I just feel kind of sick and my stomach's cramping. Maybe this will pass quickly." She saw the alarm growing in his eyes.

Anna rolled over and came up on her knees, clutching her stomach with both hands. She had a very pain–filled grimace on her face.

"I think this is the regression. Your body must be changing and that's causing the pain. I'm so sorry, cher, I didn't mean to cause you pain. I had no idea there would be pain!" She heard panic in his voice. "I'm calling my mother. She might know what to do."

In his panic his speech reverted back to a thick

Cade: Le Beau Brothers

Cajun drawl. It made her smile as she rocked back and forth on the bed, trying to ease the cramping. Add to that, dull aches began to throb throughout her joints and muscles like when her foot fell asleep.

Cade returned to her side to rub small, soothing circles on her back. All his mother knew was there would be some pain, but not too debilitating, and it would pass fairly quickly.

She rested a little easier now that the stomach cramps had let up. Her joints throughout her body were still hot and achy. And her muscles continued to contract and tighten. The sensation felt like the day after a heavy–duty workout. She had a feeling she was going to be very sore tomorrow.

"Is the pain getting any better?" he asked

"Actually it is. I can tell the change isn't over, but the cramping isn't as bad as it was."

"Can I do anything to help?"

"Just stay with me and try to be quiet. The pain control is like childbirth, I need to focus and breathe through it. If you break my concentration, I get hit with an unexpected wave, and then the level is more intense." She tried to smile, but it looked more like a grimace.

Okay, shut mouth and be invisible. Got it, Cade thought. *I'll just do what seems to sooth her and try to let her handle this.*

Anna smiled at his thoughts. He must really be upset to have left his thoughts wide open. He was normally so guarded.

Suddenly, there was a change in the sensations, and she felt her skin tightening over her newly sculpted and shaped muscles. A human shrink–wrap was the only way to explain the feeling. The thought made her giggle.

Cade wanted to ask what was funny, but, dammit, he was told to stay quiet, and that's what he would do. As he rubbed her back, he saw the changes as they happened. He wasn't completely pleased when her curves started to shrink making the soft, round body he worshipped, trimmer and a bit more lithe. He adored her extra padding, and, though he would take her any way he could get her, he would miss those extra curves. She still had an incredibly curvaceous body even with the change.

He studied her and thought, *Now she is more Marilyn Monroe and less Queen Latifah.*

It was hard to tell for sure, but in the soft lighting of the bedroom it seemed her hair had gotten lighter in color, a brighter red than it had been, and as he stroked the length he was shocked by the silky softness. He was dying to see her face, but refused to move from where he sat behind her.

I won't be the cause of her losing concentration again.

"I think the changes might be over. I don't feel any pain or tightness anymore." Her voice was almost a whisper.

"Let's give it a minute or two just to make sure before you move." As much as he wanted to wrap her in his arms, he also didn't want the pain to return.

It seemed they were in the clear. The pain and uncomfortable tightness were gone. She slowly stretched on the bed, trying out her muscles throughout her body. Surprisingly, there was no ache or soreness from over–strained muscles. She turned her attention to him, almost afraid to ask what she looked like. No mirror was visible from where she lay, and she wasn't sure what she would see.

Do I look okay?

His eyes were huge and he had a goofy expression of shock and awe on his face.

Oh, man, it's bad, isn't it?

He just shook his head, he had no words for how she looked. He stood from the bed and reached for her hand to help her up.

I want you to see for yourself.

She gave him one long, worried, intent look and walked to the full–length mirror mounted in the dressing area next to the closet. She gasped covering her mouth with her hand, glancing back and forth between her reflection and Cade's image as he stood behind her.

Is that really me?

Beautiful. Mon amour, you are stunning.

She was back to a curvy size ten like she had been in her twenties. Her hair was a brighter auburn red. Red hair tends to slowly turn brunette as you age. But now it was a beautiful shade with copper highlights throughout the lengths of soft, flowing waves. Her skin was tight and supple without the wrinkles that had started showing up in her late thirties. She could hardly believe the woman gazing back at her was really what she looked like now. She ran her palm up and down her arms amazed at the softness of her skin.

Now this, she thought as she gazed in the mirror, *was worth the pain any day of the week.*

He took her by the shoulders and turned her to face him. "I didn't believe you could be more beautiful, but now you literally take my breath away. How do you feel?"

"I can't believe that's me in the mirror. This is great, but it's going to be a long time before I can look in the mirror and not do a double take. Believe it or not, I have no residual soreness at all. I feel wonderful."

He let out a sigh. "That's a relief. I never want to go through that again. Your being in pain and my being unable to do anything about it was tearing me apart. My wolf was going insane."

Anna busted out laughing. His expression turned to confusion and hurt at her laughter. "Babe, that was nothing compared to childbirth. You'd better learn to suck it up if we have children."

His expression instantly turned to horror. "I suddenly have no desire for offspring. Someone else can supply the grandchildren."

That made her laugh even harder.

"Oh no!" she cried out.

"What!" He frantically searched for what was causing her distress.

"I don't have any clothes that will fit the new me. I can't go to the barbeque tomorrow naked. I need to buy something quick."

"Jesus, Anna, don't do that to me. You took a hundred years off my life. I'll make a few calls and get some clothes sent over. Do you have a way to measure yourself so I can tell them what size you'll need?"

"I have a cloth measuring tape in my purse."

Cade: Le Beau Brothers

Within fifteen minutes, he had a new wardrobe on its way

"I think the conversion burned up everything I ate tonight. I'm starving. Do you mind if we order room service?" She was incredibly hungry; she couldn't remember the last time she had been this starved.

"Anything you want, cher. Here's the menu. I'll call down and order whatever sounds good to you. I'm just happy to be able to take care of you again after the horrors of the conversion, even if it is only room service and new clothes."

"I feel like such a cow wanting this, but I'd really like the filet steak and the bread pudding with bourbon sauce. Oh, and a huge glass of very cold milk."

He smiled at the wistful expression on her face as she imagined the food she was ordering. "That sounds delicious. I'll order two of everything and eat with you."

Twenty minutes later a knock at the door announced dinner was served. Everything smelled better, tasted better than she had ever experienced. "This is the best food I've ever had," she moaned in food ecstasy.

"That's your new wolf senses. You will hear better, smell everything, which isn't always a good thing. Tastes will be layers now instead of a mixture of flavor, and you will have perfect night vision. All of the senses I have."

"You could've told me about this before–a girl likes to be prepared. Geez, Cade."

He laughed at her indignant scowl. "Would it have helped in any way?"

"Well, no. But still..."

"I'll try to think of anything else I failed to warn you about while I enjoy my steak," he teased.

It was already almost midnight and they had a big day tomorrow. He hustled her off to bed the minute they finished eating, and for the rest of the night the only bedroom activity on the menu was sleep. He wanted to make sure she was rested after her ordeal. Loving her would wait.

Anna woke the next morning feeling incredible. She stretched her muscles in bed, relishing the feel of having
strong, young limbs again and a flat stomach. Well, that was just the bomb as far as she was concerned.

She rolled over and snuggled against his side, rubbing herself against him like a cat, until he stirred and slowly woke up. "Who's this ravishing creature in my bed?" he peered at her through one barely open eye. Then, he pulled her in close to try to get a few more minutes of sleep.

She thumped him on the chest. "Cade Le Beau, don't you dare go back to sleep."

He chuckled with his eyes still closed as he tightened his arm around her.

She squirmed, but he had an iron grip on her and she was stuck. "I want to learn how to shift," she said in her best little girl, whiny voice.

"Maybe in an hour. I'm still tired," he teased a little more.

She let out a harrumph sound in defeat. Then she felt his chest vibrating with his silent laughter. She thumped him again.

"Violent little thing, aren't you." He laughed out loud and released her so she could get up. "I suggest we shower and eat breakfast first. Then I will help you make your first shift. Wear something loose and comfortable."

She practically threw herself out of bed and into the shower she was so excited.

He shook his head and smiled at her enthusiasm then went to brew the coffee.

Once they were both showered and breakfast finished, she was ready to try this shifting thing. He moved the furniture to the walls, creating a large open area in the middle of the room.

"Am I really going to need all this space? You never do." She studied the room speculatively.

"Better safe than sorry. This way, the furniture may avoid damage if your wolf gets frisky." There was a little too much amusement in his eyes.

"Yeah, right, you wish," she teased. "What do I need to do?"

"Close your eyes and visualize yourself as a wolf. You don't need to worry about the color and size to do it. You'll naturally become the correct wolf." He took a step out of the circle and gave her more space.

She closed her eyes, scrunching up her face as she concentrated really hard. Nothing happened. She opened her eyes feeling defeated. "I think I'm broken."

"You aren't broken, you're actually trying too hard." He grinned "Picture a wolf in your mind and imagine yourself as a wolf. Your hands are paws, you have fur and a tail."

She closed her eyes again and breathed deep to relax herself. Next thing she knew she was a little wolf tangled up in her t–shirt and running pants. She struggled to get free, but she was stuck and frankly felt ridiculous. Her wolf's head turned toward him and she tried to scowl.

Now what, Yoda?

He laughed so hard he couldn't breathe. "Imagine the clothes gone."

The petite russet wolf closed its eyes and the clothes vanished. She was so shocked she just stood blinking for a few seconds.

She was a solid, deep russet color with black and gold blended throughout the coat. In the mirror across the room her eyes glowed a vibrant green. The combination was astounding. She resembled a red fox without the white chest and tail tip.

Anna gave him the biggest wolf grin she could manage and started hopping and jumping around the room, leaping on the couch, over to the chair, on top of the dining room table. She stopped in the middle of the table, gave him a sly glance, crouched lower on her front paws, and wiggled her back end playfully. She felt her tail wag, which was just plain freaky, and spun around in a circle trying to see it.

She had him laughing so hard he was in tears.

Come and play with me, big boy. She wiggled her butt at him again.

"Mon coeur, I'd love nothing more, but two wolves in this room wouldn't be a good idea. We can go for a run at my house later. See if you can shift back. I don't want to explain a wolf in the lobby when we leave."

She concentrated, and suddenly she was a human again, but dang it, she was naked in the middle of the dining room table. She folded her arms across her breasts and scowled at him again. "How do you manage to have clothes on when you shift?" she asked in an accusing tone.

"You have to visualize yourself as human, but also exactly what you will be wearing. The reverse of shifting to the wolf, where you visualize the wolf and only fur," he explained very calmly, and for some reason his utter calm just plain pissed her off. This was serious business.

She scooted off the table and stood in the middle of the room again. She needed to visualize her clothes. Instantly she had on jeans and a t–shirt. "Are you kidding me?" She threw her arms up in the air in total annoyance.

"What? What's the problem, I thought you did quite well. She rolled her eyes, then lifted her shirt and exposed her very naked breasts. They both laughed at her lack of bra and panties.

"Let me try this again." She was determined to get this right. She imagined the wolf again and this time got it right, all wolf and no clothes. She sat down in the middle of the living room very proud of herself.

He stood and clapped for her, a one–man standing ovation.

I'm going to try shifting back with clothes this time.

He waited still standing for what seemed like minutes to her, but was really only heartbeats. Suddenly, she stood before him, human and fully clothed. They both laughed as he swung her around in a circle like a little girl.

He took her face in his hands. "I knew you could do it, mon amour."

"That was so awesome!" Her eye sparkled a brilliant green. "Should I keep practicing?"

"Not right now. We have something serious to discuss. I hope you will agree.

Chapter 14

Anna is Moving in

She accepted his outstretched hand and joined him on the couch.

"Since we're now mated, I'd like you to move to my home. I can protect you there and also teach you everything you need to learn as a shifter."

She didn't hesitate. "Do you want me to pack up my apartment today?"

As far as she was concerned, he was right. There was no reason to stay at the hotel.

"No, I'll send a crew to pack your belongings and move everything. Now, let's get ready for the party."

Anna stood in the middle of the bedroom in only her bra and panties with her hands on her hips. She'd already tried on six different outfits, and each of them had found their way to the pile of discards on the floor. She wanted to make the perfect impression, Lee jeans and white T–shirt weren't dressy enough, but she didn't want to overdress either. She finally settled on a pair of designer jeans and a designer blouse as the perfect combination of dressy casual.

V.A. Dold

While she was making her decision, he hired movers, and then stood with his arms folded over his chest waiting for her to choose what to wear. "You look good enough to eat. Let's pack up the few things here and I'll have them sent to my place."

They had her packed in less than an hour. "We have a couple of things to take care of at the front desk and then we're off," he said as he double–checked the suite for forgotten items.

"I have a unique request," he said to the bellhop captain. "I'm sending a crew to retrieve our luggage. I would like you to instruct them to deliver the bags to my home." He shook the gentleman's hand, slipping him a one hundred dollar bill.

Then they stepped to the hotel registration desk. "Good morning, Miles."

"Good morning, Cade. What can I do for you?"

"I'm returning the keys. Thank you for everything. I really appreciate your help."

"My pleasure. Anytime. Are you going to the plantation?"

"Yes, we are. My parents are having a barbeque to meet my mate."

"Congratulations! I'm so pleased you found yours. Someday I hope to be so blessed."

"He's one, too?" she whispered as they stepped from the desk.

"Yes, cher," he said chuckling as he led her to the parking garage.

Walking up to the attendant, he handed him a ticket, then grinned at her as they waited silently.

What are you up to, wolf man?

The whole time they had been together, they had

175

walked everywhere or hired taxis.

He grinned at her again and remained silent.

He's enjoying this way too much, she thought.

The growl of a motorcycle engine brought her attention to the down ramp. A sleek Harley stopped right in front of them. She stared at him, wide eyed. This she hadn't expected.

He reached into the storage compartment and handed her his extra helmet. After he was seated, he helped her get on. He raised the kickstand and turned the bike toward the exit.

She felt his wolf rumble with pleasure as she wrapped her arms around his waist and slid her hands up his stomach.

Behave yourself or we'll crash, Cade warned her teasingly.

She watched the local land and swamps speed by from the back of his bike. This was completely different than seeing it through a car window. It was raw and natural. She could imagine what it had looked like from wagons and horseback for the original settlers. Anna sighed with a little frown when they arrived.

"What's wrong?"

"Nothing. I was really enjoying the ride and hate to see it end so soon."

"There will be plenty of other chances to go for a ride, I promise." His eyes sparkled.

They were in front of a huge ranch style house with a long wraparound porch. She'd owned a house in Denver, but not one remotely this large.

"Does your whole family live here?" Surely this house was for more than just him.

V.A. Dold

"No, just li'l ol' me." He gave her a big, toothy grin.

Her boxes would be following them shortly, and she wanted to see the house before they got busy unpacking and storing her things.

"We, and by that I mean the family, own twelve hundred acres. That equals eighteen and three quarters square miles. The property runs from the river all the way into the bayou with a huge forest of mature trees covering at least half the acreage. We also own a small island about two miles further in that was originally used for trapping, hunting and fishing."

"What's it used for now?"

"A few years ago, my brothers and I renovated it into a modern cabin with all the comforts of home. It comes in handy when one of us needs a little privacy from the family."

She could tell by the tone of his voice and the sudden return of his drawl that he loved this place. As she gazed around the area and breathed in the country air, she knew to her bones she would love it, too. She finally felt like she was home for the first time in her life.

Taking her hand, he walked with her to the front door. Surprisingly, it was open with just a screen door standing in their way. He gave her a sexy, lopsided grin. "I want to do this properly."

He scooped her up, toed the door open, and carried her across the threshold. "You may not be legally Anna Le Beau yet, but in my heart, and to the shifter community as my true mate, you are Anna Le Beau in every way that counts. Welcome home, Anna Le Beau." He kissed her sweetly and then set her

177

down. "Let me show you around your new home." His smile grew larger. "I really liked saying that. 'Your home' has a great ring to it."

He took her on an extended tour of the master suite with its walk–in closets, private bath and den. They were sidetracked for a few minutes at the king–size bed. The firmness needed testing. She was able to tour the formal dining room, great room, kitchen and spare bedroom before the truck arrived. The guest wing would have to wait.

Cade had arranged for the movers to bring the boxes from her place into the house and set them in the den. He'd thought of everything for her. She stayed in the great room, out of the way, until they finished and left.

"What would you like to do first?" he asked. "I'm open for anything, I'm just thrilled you're here."

"I need to unpack a few things before they wrinkle. Give me about fifteen minutes and I'll be done."

Cade left her to unpack and place things wherever she was comfortable putting them, and he used the time to return emails and check in with Etienne about Tim. The sooner Tim was handled, the sooner he could stop worrying he was going to show up on his doorstep.

He had cancelled all his meetings for the next week so he could stay with Anna while she settled in. He worked from home, but meetings that required his attendance were a frequent event in his schedule. Next week was soon enough for more investment opportunities.

It wasn't long before she emerged from the den

looking happy and refreshed. There was a mischievous light in her eyes. "You have a jet tub large enough to swim in back there, Mr. Le Beau. I may require a guided tour of it later."

He rumbled his approval of that idea. He was all over that plan. "Between now and your tour of the jet tub, what would you like to do?"

"Are we able to shift without fear of being seen here? I would really love to see the property and try out my new wolf."

"Yes. It's very private. That's one of the reasons the family purchased it a very long time ago. Plus, the lay of the land allows for easy defense if we ever needed it. No other shifter family has ever come against the Le Beau's successfully."

"Do you fight other shifters often?" she asked with worry in her voice.

"No, we haven't had to do that for a very long time. Before you do anymore shifting you need to know the shifter rules. I learned these as a child. The Goddess decreed them as our laws when the very first shifters were created.

"Always put your mate before yourself.

"Respect another shifter's mate.

"Do nothing to expose the existence of shifters.

"Do no unnecessary harm to shifters or humans.

"Respect other nonhumans."

Anna said, "So, pretty much, respect your mate and others and keep everything a secret."

"Sure, that pretty much sums it up," he laughed. "Let me tell you a little about the property. The family homes are scattered around the estate. There is a variety of habitat ranging from forest to wetland and bayou, which provides an abundance of wildlife. Perfect for a wolf and his mate to run and play. Stay close, cher. Okay? Let's shift and have some fun."

Outside, he shifted with ease after centuries of practice. Anna was only hours new to this ability. Changing wasn't as easy as it seemed and definitely not something he'd allow her to do with an audience any time soon. The last thing he wanted was his mate naked in front of his brothers. She took five minutes and three tries, but she eventually succeeded. Shaking her body and wagging her tail, she gave him a playful little bark.

He was waiting patiently a few yards into the tree line for her to join him. Anna learned quickly that telepathic communication was very useful when in wolf form.

Are you ready, my foxy little wolf?

In answer, she rubbed up against him in a very seductive manner and batted her wolfy eyelashes at him.

Do you want to run, or reexamine the bed? Cade asked.

Run. I'll help you examine the bed later. He heard the temptation in her voice.

He was a huge wolf, much larger than a wild wolf at his 160 pounds, whereas in comparison she was a petite, delicate wolf of only one hundred pounds. Even though he was much bigger, he knew she would be able to handle herself in her wolf form. He didn't envy the wolf stupid enough to underestimate her.

Cade took off running, relishing the feel of his wolf's efficiency of movement. The wolf's body was streamlined and made for hunting and tracking over long distances. Anna darted in and out of trees and the thick bayou plant growth testing her agility.

After a short distance he stopped. Sniffing the air, he scanned for dangers before beginning the tour for his mate.

Cher, when you run as a wolf, always stop every so often and scan for any danger.

He watched her as she sniffed as well to get the scent of what the natural aroma would be so she would be able to smell the difference if there were danger.

Excellent, head to your left. I want to show you the river.

She was amazed at how quickly she covered distances in this form. Within minutes they stood on the riverbank. She smelled the damp earth and wet decomposing leaves and brush. The Spanish moss hanging from the trees had a musty odor and the water was rich with a mixture of layers all its own. She craned her neck to see up and down the river, scanning for danger as she had been instructed to do. *All clear*, she announced happily.

He gave her a little yip of encouragement and they set off along the riverbank to the far eastern property line.

Can you smell the other shifters' scents that have come this way before us?

Yes, I think I can make out four different wolf scents.

Exactly, that's what I smell as well. They are my brothers' and father's scents. In time you'll be able to tell them apart. If you smell a heavy line of scent like this, you have reached a boundary. We often patrol the edge and the repeat traffic creates a heavy scent line.

Cade: Le Beau Brothers

Cade increased his speed, with Anna close on his tail. Their paws hit the ground in a steady beat soothing to her wolf soul. She loved the feel of the wind ruffling her fur. The sensation was invigorating.

As they approached the north end of the estate, he slowed to a walk, lifting his nose to the breeze as he scented the air. She mimicked his actions and caught the enticing aroma of game. The scent made her nose twitch with excitement. Her ears perked up as her eyes scanned the surrounding area, expecting to locate the animal with the delicious scent. They crouched down and remained very quiet, waiting. A twig snap to the right seconds before a gorgeous doe stepped into the clearing. She was magnificent!

They quietly watched her feed for a few minutes before he signaled to her it was time to move on. He led her along the northern border edging the bayou to the western side where the forest was the thickest.

It would be a ball to play hide and seek around here.

He responded, *you can try, but I'd just sniff you out and pin your sexy furriness to the ground before I had my way with you.*

Oh really? You think you can pin me, huh?

Damn straight, cher.

The challenge was on, she swished her tail and shot like a rocket back to the house. She surprised him with the speed in her little body.

Next time he'd think twice before laying down a challenge, she thought.

She beat him by a nose to the front door, skidding to a stop before she went right through the screen door. That was close.

He shifted easily to his human form and sat on the porch swing waiting for her to shift back. He had said getting good would take years and a lot of practice to be able to do a change as easily as he did, and she was convinced he was right.

I hate you right now.

"No, you don't, you love me. You're just frustrated. Relax, clear your mind and visualize your human form. Oh, and don't forget your underwear."

She stopped what she was doing and glared at him, letting a low growl escape.

I'm not amused.

Cade barked out a laugh.

Three minutes and three tries later they walked back into the house.

Chapter 15

Meeting the parents

Anna took a deep breath–she could do this. She was sure his parents would be wonderful people, plus she had already met Stefan and Marcus. How bad could meeting the parents be? She was dressed, so all she had to do was check her hair and face.

"Should I quickly make something to bring?" She was a bit panicked. She had nothing to offer at the party! She felt like such an idiot for not being prepared.

"Don't worry, cher, they know we're newly mated and you just moved in. They're not expecting you to bring anything but me." He pulled her in for a kiss, and looked very pleased with himself.

He took her by the hand as they walked the three acres to the main house. She was nervous and she knew he was able to sense it. He often told her his wolf hated its mate being unsure or apprehensive in any way, and instinctively he always tried to comfort her.

The instant Cade rounded the corner, she heard a high pitched squeal of delight.

That's my mother. She's very excited I've claimed

you. Be prepared for a hug and a lot of squealing, he warned.

She covered her mouth with her hand to hide her grin as he was almost knocked over by his round little mother. He was caught in a tight hug, rolling his eyes at his brothers over her shoulder. They both snickered at his predicament.

"Hi, Mom. I love you too but you're squeezing a little too tight. I kind of need air here. And as soon as I can breathe again I will introduce you to my mate."

His mother loosened her hold, blushing and appeared a bit embarrassed. Emma took a step back and smoothed her skirt nervously. Anna thought her exuberance was sweet.

"Mom, this is my Anna. Anna, this is Emma, my mother." He quickly stepped back.

Be prepared, cher, your hug is coming…

His mother appeared like one would expect, a combination gypsy voodoo priestess to look. She had long, dark, shiny hair and almost black eyes. She wore a turban looking thing wrapped around her head combined with a peasant blouse and broom skirt in the craziest pattern she had ever seen. Her multitude of necklaces, bracelets, and earrings created tinkling sounds. Somehow the outfit worked together and she was enchanting.

The assessment only took her about two heartbeats, but apparently even a few seconds was too much for Emma to withstand. She swooped in and had her in the tightest hug she had ever experienced.

"Mother, I think you need to loosen your hold on my mate so she can take a breath." Cade said as Anna gasped for air.

Cade: Le Beau Brothers

"I'm sorry, Anna, I forget my strength and tend to squeeze too hard when I'm excited."

She smiled a genuinely warm smile at her new mother–in–law. She was sweet, loving, and a truly caring person. How could anyone not love her? "There's nothing to apologize for. It's wonderful to receive such a warm welcome." To prove her point, she grabbed Emma and gave her a bear hug in return, which had his mother beaming with happiness.

Have I told you today how perfect you are?
No, I don't believe you have.
I'll be sure to tell you all about it later.

She had to work at keeping her facial expression bland. She was still a little shy about public shows of affection in front of his family.

He placed his hand at the small of her back and steered her to the other end of the patio where Stephan and Marcus stood. "Where's Dad?"

"Your father's making sure the steaks are seasoned to perfection and won't join us until he is satisfied with his artistic gastronomic creation," Emma said while gesturing dramatically for effect.

The boys chuckled and shook their heads.

Huh, she thought, *must be a family joke.*

Cade left her with his brothers while he made them cocktails at the bar. She was looking forward to a tall, cold gin and tonic. Her nerves cried out for a drink. Meeting parents was stressful no matter how nice they were.

He came back and wrapped her up in not only his arms, but his warmth and love. She needed that right now. She actually sighed a little in relief, which made Emma smile even larger.

V.A. Dold

*****

Emma Le Beau was over the moon seeing Cade's happiness, and she already adored his lovely mate. Their plan to help him meet her had worked perfectly. She was practically dancing in place waiting for her husband, Isaac, to join them and meet her himself.

She decided now would be a good time to bring up the subject of Anna's friends back in Denver. Perhaps she could steer the conversation so she would bring up her friend, Rose. It would be fairly easy to turn the discussion, so the idea of inviting her here for a visit could be offered.

"Anna, do you stay in touch with any of your friends in Denver? You have been here for what, six months? I'm sure you miss your friends from there."

"My sons still live there, and my very best friend, Rose, is there as well. I miss all of them terribly, but they have jobs and lives so I cope with phone calls and Skype."

"You and Cade have a big house with all those extra rooms. You should invite them to visit soon," Emma suggested.

Anna got a thoughtful expression and nodded her head. "That's a great idea. The next time I speak with them I will mention visiting. John and Thomas still need to meet Cade. Since they are self–employed, I am sure they can make time to come. Rose might be a little more difficult. Her position keeps her so busy she hardly ever takes a vacation day."

Emma knew the situation would work itself out. With the seed planted all she had to do was sit back

187

and wait. "I wonder what's keeping Isaac." She quickly changed the subject–best to not be too obvious.

*****

As if on cue, Isaac walked out the patio door. First thing he did was put his arm around his mate, giving her a quick peck on the cheek. Emma excitedly whispered to him, bringing his attention to Anna. As the alpha, Isaac was extremely dominant. He sensed, as he locked eyes with his new daughter, his intensity made her nervous. He had no intention of making her uneasy in anyway, his nature was simply part of the beast. Isaac's sharp vision picked up on her trembling hands, causing the ice in her glass to tinkle quietly. His son reacted to her fear by tightening his arm around her protectively and sending him a glare of reprimand.

Isaac smiled at her warmly to calm her. He wanted to ease her anxiety. He tended to forget how intense he appeared to others.

"Anna, welcome to our family. We're so pleased to have you as a new daughter." Isaac purposely called her daughter instead of daughter–in–law to announce her place in the family to everyone. She would always be a family member, not simply a mate who came in from the outside. This was a huge honor he was giving her.

He stepped forward to Cade and Anna, clapping him on his back before pulling her into a warm, fatherly embrace. As he released her, he gave her a light kiss on the cheek as any parent would give a daughter.

"Now back to the important task of grilling these steaks," he said with a warm gleam in his eyes.

*****

Anna let the stress of meeting the family wash away. Now that Isaac was busy with the grill she took a moment to study him. She saw where Cade inherited a lot of his features. His father was tall, maybe an inch taller than him. They were both very handsome with long, wavy dark hair. He also had the same well–built body with wide shoulders, muscular chest, and an abdomen that tapered into a fit, narrow waist. Even though he was intimidating as hell, he had warm, expressive, brilliant green eyes. She really liked his eyes.

His family made her feel like a member, not a stranger joining them, and she appreciated their generosity.

She went into the kitchen to help Emma with last–minute food preparations and table setting. As she was placing the silverware, she saw a wolf's tail hanging off the end of the couch in the great room.

Babe, is there another wolf here I haven't met?

That's Simon. He remains in wolf form most of the time. We're helping him recover from his four years in the Marines. He may not join us tonight; the family leaves the choice to be in human form up to him.

She felt a strong draw to go to Simon, and before she knew what she was doing she'd walked over to the sleeping wolf. Not wanting to startle him, she spoke before she tried to touch him. "Hello, Simon, I'm

Cade: Le Beau Brothers

Anna. Cade's mate. May I touch you?"

Cade and his mother had followed her as far as the doorway when they saw her walking in Simon's direction.

The wolf made a small harrumph sound and opened his eyes. She squatted next to the couch about ten inches from his face waiting for his permission. He reached forward, stretching his neck toward her, licking her cheek. His wolfy hello made her giggle and she took it as a yes.

Simon rumbled, he sounded like Cade when he was pleased or content. Taking that as a good sign she stroked him and scratched behind his ears. Her touch must have felt good to him. His wolf continued the soft rumble of satisfaction in his chest, as close to a purr as a wolf could get from what Cade had told her. He adjusted his position on the couch, which allowed her to reach his other side. He didn't seem to want her to stop.

When she heard Isaac calling for everyone to be seated she whispered, "I'll come back after dinner if you would like."

As everyone was seated, a hush fell over the family as all heads turned to the doorway behind her. She turned to see what was causing this reaction. Simon slowly walked to her seat. It appeared as though he strained to walk those few steps as he tightened his jaw determinedly. He extended his hand to her in greeting. "Welcome, Anna," was all he said, but those two words spoke volumes. She gave him her hand and remained very still as he raised it to gently brush his lips across her knuckles. As he released her hand, he turned to Cade. "You have a lovely mate, brother.

She's a treasure." Then he turned and walked back to the couch taking wolf form again.

The dinner was very quiet as everyone digested what just happened. She wanted to know what had put the family into such a reflective state, but she knew someone would explain everything to her later when they were finished.

She offered to help clean up after dinner, but Emma pulled her aside and requested she sit with Simon again. She was helping him and that was more important. She wasn't sure exactly how she was helping, but if this was what Emma wanted, she'd do it.

Cade was bursting with pride for his mate. Her empathy and care of others had no bounds.

He quietly sat in a chair remaining in the shadows of the room, not wanting to disturb her in any way. Today had been the first time anyone had seen Simon interact with another person who wasn't blood related to him, and Anna had something to do with that. Somehow her touch had drawn his brother out of whatever dark hole he was trapped in.

There was no jealousy over his mate stroking his brother, both he and his wolf instinctively sensed her attentions were a form of healing and not romantic in any way. He wasn't sure what was happening between Simon and his mate, he only knew the results were profound. She was helping him return to them with just her touch. Even his wolf sat silently watching in awe of their mate.

Cade focused on her hands. They were placed strategically on Simon's head and chest. He would bet money she was unaware of the way she intuitively

Cade: Le Beau Brothers

reached for the perfect position. A shifter's wolf resided mainly in his thoughts and heart, a virtual second soul in the body. She had unerringly touched Simon's wolf within without realizing it.

He would have to ask his mother about what exactly was happening with his mate. He had a feeling, that with her training as a healer, she would have a theory. He was convinced she had tapped into her special shifter gift by accident.

What an amazing gift to have.

Anna had sat on the floor next to the couch and placed her hands gently on Simon's head and chest. She just held them there for a long time. As she touched him, she felt a mild heat radiating from her palms. The sensation was startling at first, but the warmth wasn't painful. In truth, it actually felt soothing, so she remained calm and went with it. Simon started his low contented rumble again and relaxed under her hands.

The house had become very quiet. She realized she must have sat with Simon longer than she thought. Slowly, her hands began to cool. Not sure what she was doing, she took the temperature change as a sign to stop. Simon rolled off the couch and lowered himself to the floor next to her. He laid his head in her lap for a moment, gave her hand a little lick, then rose and padded down the hall and out of sight.

Without a word Cade took her hand to help her stand so they could join his family around the fire pit in the yard. His brothers and parents were talking softly as they approached. Two chairs waited for their arrival.

Emma spoke first. "How did it go, Anna?"

"I'm not sure what you mean?" She looked to Cade for answers, but he appeared as curious as she was.

Emma leaned toward her and took her hand. "You are a healer. From what I saw today, you can restore another's health with healing energy. From the surprise on your face, I'm guessing you never knew you had the gift. Natural healers use energy, herbs, crystals, essential oils, and many natural elements to heal others. Did your hands heat as you touched Simon?"

"How'd you know?" she gasped and put her hand to her heart, reaching for Cade with the other.

"I and many of my friends are trained in the healing arts, but you, my dear Anna, are a rare natural healer. You don't need training, you instinctively do what is needed for the injured person." She smiled sweetly.

"Training will make you even better at what you do naturally, and I can teach you the herbs and other tools of healing. I can mentor you if you'd like to work with me." She rubbed her hands together as if she were anticipating training her. "I've dreamed of having a daughter to pass my knowledge to, but Isaac and I were never blessed with one until now."

Cade added, "My mother comes from a long line of gypsies in the old country, and trained in the voodoo arts and religion in this country. Her knowledge is vast and her power is off the charts." He squeezed Anna's hand, then added, "My mother, also, bears the mark of the new moon."

His remark snapped Emma to attention. "She bears the mark?" she whispered reverently.

"Yes, I have one on my shoulder."

"Even better." Emma became very quiet and wore an expression of deep thought.

"Perhaps it's a good time to explain to Anna what's wrong with Simon," Isaac volunteered.

The men exchanged glances, each nodded once. Cade began, "wolves are a very physical animal. They require a lot of contact with other wolves or humans. The same applies to us. You may have noticed I touch you often even if only a light touch on the shoulder and stroke of your hair. That's all a part of it."

"Simon joined the Marines four years ago without thoroughly thinking it through. In the service he was primarily surrounded by other Marines. Touching each other isn't encouraged. Simon found himself rapidly regressing into himself as a survival response," Isaac explained.

"Whenever he had leave or was at a base function where he could socialize, he'd find a way to get human touch. If there was a dance with women for him to touch and hold on the dance floor, he'd dance all night. If there were no social events planned, he'd hire a prostitute–not for sex, but to simply give him a body massage and stroke his hair. Overseas where he was stationed, ladies of the night are in massage parlors and there is a price list posted on the wall. You would think men were ordering fast food and the women were a cheap meal," Marcus said with disgust.

"He went as far as to get an extensive tattoo on his back of a wolf because the work took the artist days and days to do, all the while touching him. He said the wolf he tattooed on his back would come to him in his dreams and lay beside him quietly each night to comfort him. So he drew the wolf and had the sketch done as a tattoo." Marcus spoke very quietly as he described how his brother fought to cope.

"He managed to remain sane, but he has regressed into himself so deeply, we're struggling to help him find his way back. We each take time every day to sit with him and just stroke him. Our attempts have been helping a little, but what you did today was extraordinary," Stefan said. "Your gift is the most amazing thing I've ever seen."

"We can't thank you enough for your healing today, Anna." Isaac's voice hitched with emotion.

"I'd like to make a request of you and Cade if I may. I'm reluctant to ask this of you, but we are in dire need." Emma sobbed. Isaac took her hand to offer what comfort he could as they sat in the circle. "Normally I'd never ask a newly–mated wolf to spend extensive time with a wolf who is not their mate, but I'm afraid I must. Would you be willing to come by each day and do a healing session with Simon?"

She looked to Cade. *I'm sorry if this is difficult for you, but I truly can't deny this impulse in me. It's like an ache in my bones. As long as he's in this condition I won't be able to stop myself. I was literally drawn into the room today almost against my will. This need to heal that I didn't even know I had has a mind of its own.*

I love you, Anna, I'll always provide whatever you need. If that's healing Simon, then I'll come with you every day and lend you strength and support to heal him. Both I and my wolf understand this is all about healing. We feel no threat to you or to our mating bond.

Cade: Le Beau Brothers

She wanted to jump in his lap and kiss him senseless for his understanding and support. She looked everyone in the eye one by one and lastly reached for Emma's hand. "Emma, both Cade and I are happy to do whatever we can to help Simon. I'll be back every day until he no longer needs me."

Emma cried with relief. Isaac held her in his lap and rocked her as the men and Anna silently walked to their houses on the estate leaving their parents to collect themselves.

Anna and Cade walked in silence, both deep in thought. So much had happened in one short day.

Without speaking, he led her to the master bath and started the water. He added some lovely floral scented bath salts and a rolled up towel to tuck behind her neck. She curiously stood back and watched him as he worked effortlessly, as if he'd done this a hundred times.

"Run a woman's bath often, do you?" she jokingly teased him.

He cleared his throat. "Not hardly. But I've watched you closely these past few days and this seems to be what you would enjoy. Did I do it wrong?"

"Actually, you did it perfectly." She brushed her hand down his back and over his delectable ass as he bent over to test the water.

"You're a terrible woman to torture me so," he said right before he splashed her playfully. "Now get naked and enjoy your bath."

Anna hesitated. "Aren't you getting in, too?"

"Not this time. I want you to take a little time to totally relax. You've had a lot to deal with today, and this is all for you."

He never ceased to surprise and amaze her. One minute he was an alpha male growling at everyone and the next he was running her a bath because he thought she needed a little 'me' time.

Cade went to the great room to give her privacy; he needed to check his messages. Etienne had called, they had been following Tim and he would begin monitoring him tonight in preparation of his modification. He was relieved the danger to his mate would be handled soon.

He heard Anna enjoying her bath–she had really needed the relaxation time. Sometimes she didn't know when to stop giving of herself and take a personal break. Well, he would make sure to take care of her if she wouldn't do it herself. She was too selfless sometimes and he didn't want her to exhaust herself.

He glanced up as she entered the room; he'd have to call Etienne tomorrow. She was in the slinky silk negligee he bought for her with the new wardrobe. The sight of her in the almost see–through gown had him breathing heavily.

How'd I ever get so lucky?

I have no idea, she teased.

She did a slow circle for him, stopping with her back turned. He knew she was giving him a good long look on purpose. Glancing over her shoulder, she gave him a sultry wink. Then she completed the turn. He had to force himself to remain seated.

She grabbed both arms of the chair he was sitting in as she stood between his thighs. Slowly she leaned forward giving him a really good look at her cleavage. He growled when she stopped just out of his reach for

Cade: Le Beau Brothers

a kiss. Little tease.

Before she was able to move away from his chair, he snatched her into his lap and devoured her lips. "You're a terrible tease, but I like it," Cade whispered in her ear.

That made her giggle.

He stood with her still in his arms and went to the master suite to re–inspect the bed.

A man can never be too careful about the quality of his bed, he thought, as he made love to his mate.

Twice.

V.A. Dold

Chapter 16

Etienne

Etienne Delacour was monitoring Tim twenty–four seven. Cade had asked him to modify Tim's memories and desires toward his ex–wife. To make him want to leave her alone, move out of Louisiana, and be happy about it.

Tim was harassing Anna. Cade wanted it stopped before the situation became deadly. Combine an unstable ex–husband and the local mob and you had a cocktail for pain and suffering. That was not to be allowed.

He decided it would be wise to investigate the little beast of a human. He and three of his family followed Tim for the next two days. His best tech guy bugged Tim's apartment, tapped his phone, and put a tracker on him.

It didn't take long to find out Tim was in deep with the mob. Tim was seen going to the casino every night after work and not leaving until the early morning hours. Upon Etienne's orders, the vampires became invisible and followed him into the casino the next night.

199

Cade: Le Beau Brothers

*****

Tim sat himself at a craps table and immediately began losing money. Based on his betting pattern, this idiot had no idea how to play the game. Combine ignorance with plain old bad luck and you have Tim James, loser.

They watched him in silence as he racked up fifty thousand dollars in bad debt to the casino. Both vampires shook their heads, this idiot was a dead man. About fifteen minutes later two thugs came to the table and dragged Tim into a back room. The vampires followed behind and slipped into the room before the door closed. Tim was roughly tossed into a metal folding chair. He hung his head as if by not being able to see the men in the room, he would be safe.

"Tim, it's come to my attention you have fifty in markers. How do you intend to pay that back?" The mob boss tipped his head to stare Tim in the eye. When he didn't answer, the thug behind him grabbed him by the hair and forced his head up.

"I don't have the money on me," Tim stammered.

"My boys here tell me you have a wife, that you have been married for a very long time. Perhaps if I give your wife special accommodations for a while you'll suddenly find my fifty to get her back?"

One of the thugs tossed an eight by ten picture of Anna onto the table. The photo appeared to have been taken in Jackson Square. Tim remained silent. He didn't correct them regarding his marital status, he would let them believe Anna was a good target and maybe that would save his ass. He was letting them think this would work.

The boss caressed the photo. "For a woman in her forties she's rather pretty, and I love a woman with extra cushion for the pushin. I think she'll enjoy being tied to my bed, don't you?"

The boss turned to his men. "Get him out of my sight. If he doesn't pay within forty–eight hours, grab my new sex toy."

Etienne's men gave him a complete report on the situation Tim had gotten himself into. The bastard was purposely dragging Anna into it as well. Both Tim and the casino boss would need to be dealt with quickly. Give the idiot a couple drinks and he didn't shut up. Cade was going to kill this moron.

Etienne left a message on Cade's phone that he had news and would call again in the morning.

*****

At eight a.m. the phone rang. "Cade, Etienne here." The vamp was always a man of few words. Something he knew Cade appreciated.

"What do you have?" He had answered the phone in the kitchen and Anna could walk in any second.

"He owes fifty. If the money is not paid today they will come for Anna. And, Cade, the kingpin threatened her sexually." He spoke with sympathy in his voice. He hated telling his friend his mate was threatened.

Cade crushed the glass he held in his hand. He was growling dangerously into the phone. Etienne knew the anger was not aimed at him and waited for Cade to collect himself.

Cade: Le Beau Brothers

"I'll make the payment personally and send them a much needed message. Thank you, my friend. Please proceed with Tim's redirection as soon as you can. Also, feel free to feed, I'd like him watched indefinitely, and your mind–reading ability to link to those you have bitten will be very useful. I don't trust this punk to not get Anna into danger again."

Etienne laughed. "My pleasure, Cade. I will try to not flash my fangs or let my eyes grow red while I am looking him in the eye." There was a click and Etienne was gone.

He knew Etienne would do exactly that. He meant to scare the shit out of Tim. There was nothing he hated more than a coward that used a woman as a shield. The man was getting off easy as a favor to him. Normally his treatment of vermin like Tim was a bit more deadly.

He set his phone on the counter and leaned on both hands as he hung his head and tried to calm down. He wanted to be composed when he saw Anna; if she saw him like this his eyes would alarm her.

He heard her unpacking in the bedroom. Good, that would keep her busy while he went to the casino. "Cher, I need to run to the city for an hour or so. Do you need anything while I'm there?"

"No, not that I can think of. Will you be home for lunch?" She sounded like her head was deep inside a box.

"I'm sure I'll be home in plenty of time." He brushed his hand down her lower back and continued south.

She rose from the box, a glint in her eye and one eyebrow cocked. Her expression broke his foul mood instantly. One sweet kiss and he was out the door. He wanted this over with. Like yesterday.

*****

Cade didn't bother to knock. Scum like these men didn't deserve that kind of respect. He threw the door open and smashed the kingpin to the desktop before his goons blinked once. "You'll listen very closely. I'll only say this once. Anna James is mine. She is under my personal protection. If you or any of your people even look in her general direction, if you hire someone to cause her harm, if you look at her or any of her friends or family sideways, I will rip your gut open and feast on your entrails while you watch. I'll ensure you remain alive for a very long time as I slowly dissect you one organ at a time. You will not die well."

He threw the fifty thousand on the desk. "Do you understand everything I have said?"

Everyone stood frozen, afraid to even breathe.

"Speak now! Yes or no!" He was close to losing control of his wolf completely.

"Yes! Yes! I understand." The boss frantically glanced from Cade's hand to his face.

Back and forth.

The leader of the mob was the only one who saw his hand shift into a wolf's paw with wicked, deadly claws that flexed and dug deeply into his skin. In a split second Cade snapped the man's arm, causing the bone to pierce through the skin and the arm to hang at a sickening angle. The agonized screams were no doubt heard all the way to the casino.

Leaning down he whispered, "I know what you intended to do to my mate." The sound of finger bones snapping echoed in the room and the mob boss screamed again. "Speak of her again in such a manner and I will rip off your dick and shove the pathetic thing down your throat."

He roughly shoved the evil scum from him and turn to exit the office.

"Um, boss...Mr. Comeaux," one of the goons said from across the room.

Panting in pain the mobster sat up and glared at the man.

"We have a problem," the goon continued.

Cade's head spun around and he latched onto the goon's throat. "What kind of problem?" he snarled.

"Jonesy and Ralph followed you from the hotel and are already staking out your place. With you not there..." he squeaked in terror.

Instantly Cade was gone. He moved so fast no one was able to see him actually leave. To them, he simply vanished.

*****

Anna was unpacking her bathroom boxes when her old monthly friend returned. She realized she needed feminine hygiene items she hadn't needed for the past couple years. Cade would be embarrassed if she sent him shopping for what she needed, so she grabbed her purse to go to town. He had a sedan in the garage and the keys hung by the door so she was set.

As she pulled out of the driveway, the two men who were watching her followed. They kept a distance behind her to not draw attention to themselves. Within a few minutes she pulled into the small corner store a few miles from the plantation. Unaware of her shadow she grabbed her purse and got out of her car. As she was locking it, a man grabbed her from behind and hauled her backwards into a waiting van.

The last thought she had before losing consciousness was, *these men are dead when Cade gets a hold of them.*

*****

UGH! What's that awful smell!
Anna awoke and jerked her face from the offending rancid mattress that her nose was buried in. It all came rushing back, she had been grabbed from behind at the convenience store.
Okay, where am I and how many of them are there?
Slowly she turned her head enough to see the room hoping the movement wouldn't be noticed by her captors. It looked like an old, rickety cabin. The room held the single bed she was on and one wooden chair. There was a window with ragged curtains that had seen much better days.
I think I can fit through that window if I can open it.
She listened for sounds coming from the other side of the bedroom door. She heard a television, but couldn't tell who was behind the door without opening it. She gave her new heightened wolf senses a try.

Pressing her nose close to the crack, she took a deep breath. Two of them.

Try to open the door a crack or attempt the window? Window first.

Quietly she tiptoed to the window and examined it carefully. There was no lock. With only a short drop to the ground, this would be doable. She would need to cross about twenty feet of open yard before she had the safety of the trees. If she could open it without alerting anyone, she could escape.

Taking a deep breath, she braced her feet and pushed on the frame. It rose only an inch with a deafening screech, then jammed.

Shit.

Scrambling furniture and running footsteps were heard seconds before the door slammed open. Two very large men filled the doorway.

"What do you think you're doing, little missy," the dark haired one asked.

"Yeah, Ralph, we're in the middle of the bayou, where did she think she could go?" the blonde added.

She had to think fast. They stepped into the room and advanced on her. She followed her new wolf instincts and shifted. Apparently stress and dire need helped in the shifting process because she did it perfectly the first try.

The goons stopped in their tracks, shocked by the sight of her shifting into a wolf. They must have known about shifters because that moment of hesitation ended very quickly. Ralph dove for her but she scrambled between his legs and rammed the blonde out of the way as she made for the next room.

She skidded to a halt, stuck in the main room of the cabin.

Well hell, now what. I can't open the front door without hands.

Ralph and his buddy were at the other end of the room and she was backed against her unusable exit.

"Jonesy, you go left and I will go right. Grab her and we'll tie her up," Ralph said.

As they slowly closed in, a cell phone rang. She glanced to where it lay on the table next to a gun.

That's it! If I can contain these two idiots, I can call Cade. These buffoons are no match for my wolf.

She waited until Jonesy reached for her. Without warning she latched onto his arm, biting as hard as she could. Anna shook her head roughly for good measure.

Jonesy howled in pain.

With her wolf focused on Jonesy, she couldn't see Ralph but she heard him coming at her. As he tried to grab her around the neck, she released Jonesy and spun away from Ralph's grip.

Jonesy was ass–planted on the floor cradling his bloody and torn arm.

One down, one to go, she thought. *Come and get me, big guy.*

Ralph made another grab for her and she clamped down on his leg. Fabric ripping and pain filled screams were loud in the little room.

Anna waited for the goons to stop yowling before she started snarling and growling. She wanted them to be paying close attention so she could herd them into the corner. To avoid her deadly jaws, both men crab walked backwards to the exact place she wanted.

Cade: Le Beau Brothers

She stood next to the table with the cell phone and gun. Taking a deep breath, she visualized herself human and clothed in jeans and T–shirt. A second later Anna, the human, stood before them. Snatching up the gun, she held it on the goons and with an audible click flipped the safety off.

*****

"Sit your butts in the chairs, boys," she said indicating the only two wooden chairs in the room. There was a duffle bag on the couch. Rummaging through, she found an adequate length of rope to tie them to the chairs.

Jonesy whined like a wuss as she pulled his hands behind him and tied them tightly.

Ralph glared at her. She could tell he was trying to think his way out of the situation. "In case this gun isn't incentive enough for you to behave yourself, Ralph, I can always bring the wolf back." Raising her eyebrows, she gave him a pointed look.

Scowling he put his hands behind his back so she could tie him.

After picking up the cell phone, she dialed Cade. As the phone rang she smacked her forehead with the heel of her palm.

I could have used telepathy.

"Hello, Cade Le Beau."

"Cade, It's me. I was kidnapped and could use a little assistance."

"Thank God! Where are you? Are you hurt?"

"No, I'm not hurt. These two idiots are bleeding pretty good though. I have them tied to a couple chairs and they conveniently provided me with a gun and phone. But I have no idea where I am. Hold on."

She looked at Ralph and Jonesy. "Where are we, boys?"

Ralph sneered at her. "As if we are going to tell you."

The conversation stopped and a few seconds later a wolf started snarling. Ralph quickly gave up the cabin's location when she focused on his crotch.

"Did you hear that or should I repeat it?" she asked Cade.

Laughing, "I got it, cher. I will be there in about thirty minutes by boat. Do you need me to bring you anything?"

"No, I'm good. Just hurry. I love you, Cade," she whispered to him.

"I love you too, Anna. I will be there before you know it."

Stefan sat across the room from Cade. They had been trying to figure out where she was being held. "Did she get free of them?" he asked.

"Yeah, she seems to have them as her captives now," he chuckled.

"Damn, I need a woman like her. That's kind of hot," Stefan laughed.

"Follow me in your boat. Once I get Anna out of there, you can take care of the men."

"My pleasure. Do I get to bite them, too?" Stefan asked jokingly.

"Do as you please, just deliver them to the casino when you are done having fun. Be sure to make an impression on the boss when you return his trash."

Cade: Le Beau Brothers

*****

Thirty–five minutes later, Anna heard boats docking. Boots thundered across the dock moments before Cade and Stefan came through the door. Both men doubled over laughing at the sight of Anna sitting on top of the dining room table twirling her gun like Annie Oakley. Ralph and Jonesy were clearly not amused.

She hopped off the table and jumped into Cades arms. He held her tight, then let her slip to the floor. "I was ready to come in here and kick some butt. You ruined all my fun," he teased.

Stefan shook his head, "I can't wait to hear this story."

She and Cade left as Stefan took possession of the goons. Cade cuddled her close under his arm all the way home. If she hadn't been so calm and had the men tied when he arrived, his wolf would have killed those men. They had her to thank for their lives.

Once they were safely home, she told him the entire story. She was especially proud of her shift during the daring escape.

When Stefan returned from his come–to–Jesus meeting with the boss, she retold the story to him. She was so animated as she told it, she had the men laughing until they couldn't breathe.

"I don't think we made any friends at the casino today," Stefan told them when the laughter died down. "We will have to be on guard against retaliation for a while."

"Tomorrow call a meeting with Dad and the men. Fill them in on the details and schedule around–the–clock border patrol and security until further notice. Next time it may be Mom they try to snatch."

*****

Etienne had an impressive antebellum mansion. More than one billionaire had attempted to purchase his home, but that would never happen. Two and a half glorious stories of southern history. Immense columns held up a hipped roof that created the wraparound covered porch completely around the first and second levels. Entering the front door, a visitor was transported back in time.

Etienne had every classic touch and only the finest furnishings money could buy. He had shared this place with a beloved human woman once, had given her his heart and soul. The happiest day of his existence had been the day she agreed to be his queen and join him as a vampire. His happiness had been short–lived. A mob of humans caught his queen when she was away from the mansion and ended her existence.

Cade had come upon the scene and tried to stop the horrific killing, but not before it was too late. He hadn't been able to save her, but he had held her and comforted her until the end. He then carried her in his arms, walking the entire five miles to the mansion to return her body to him. He would always owe Cade for that kindness and show of loyal friendship.

Thus Etienne had no problem sending his right–hand man to collect Tim to bring him to the estate he called home. It was daylight, but the sun wouldn't have stopped him. He was an ancient and no longer held captive by that burning ball in the sky. He was considered the king of the vampires in New Orleans, and it was simply below him to collect vermin like Tim.

*****

Tim James had been held at the police station for twenty–four hours before being released. He had no idea Cade had arranged for the charges to be dropped in order to get Tim out of the state and away from Anna.

Etienne had waited until he was free and unsuspecting to make his move.

Tim was exiting the courtyard of his apartment building. He hadn't bothered to observe his surroundings, not expecting danger at seven in the morning. Wrong.

In less than four steps, a hand gripped his arm tightly as another hand covered his nose and mouth with a cloth. Generally a vampire didn't require the use of chloroform to subdue a victim, but Etienne wanted him delivered whole and unharmed. The harming would be Etienne's pleasure.

The vampire sighed as he grumbled, "I really wanted to hurt this piece of trash. Etienne is going to owe me for this."

Tim was tossed carelessly into the trunk of a sedan and driven to the mansion. There was little care taken in avoiding bumps and potholes. The vampires knew of the beast's treatment of Cades mate. There'd be no mercy for him as long as he insisted on remaining in New Orleans. If the idiot had half a brain, he'd move immediately. There were many hungry friends of the Le Beau's wanting a taste of this human.

It was the basement, which held the most interesting aspects of Etienne's home. A series of cells and torture rooms lined the space. Etienne was either a person's best ally or worst nightmare. If you were on his enemy list or an enemy of a friend, you had better run far and fast. If caught, the situation wouldn't end well. Tim was roughly dragged by his one good arm to a basement cell and tossed in. He was left in a heap to sleep off the chloroform on the cold stone floor.

When Tim woke, he would have no idea where he was, if it was day or night. His first thought would be the mob had grabbed him. All he would be able to do was shiver in the dark stone room waiting for the torture to begin.

Little did he know his debt had been paid and a much more dangerous creature held him. At some point a single bare bulb hanging from the ceiling turned on. Etienne enjoyed this part, his victim, Tim, could now see he was in a solid brick, square room. The only way in or out was a three–inch thick solid wood door. He was screwed.

Etienne left Tim to wait alone in the bare room with no furniture, no windows, only the bare bulb hanging from the ceiling. The wondering of what would happen to him was its own kind of torture. What must have felt like hours to Tim had passed as he pounded on the door, yelling for help. Begging for mercy.

Cade: Le Beau Brothers

The click of the door announced Etienne as he calmly entered the cell. Tim backed away until he was flat against the wall. Etienne knew he was a striking figure, at six foot four with wide shoulders, lean hips and muscles that seemed to ripple even as he stood still. He was ruggedly handsome with a neat ponytail of coal black hair that ran halfway down his back. Too many women over the century's had raved about his beauty for him to not know how humans viewed him. When you were as ancient as he was, beauty was much more than physical features, they meant nothing to him anymore.

Most women found him irresistible. Most men were terrified of him. Etienne preferred it that way. He radiated menace and evil on purpose. Vampires had the ability to affect the vibes they emitted. Normally Etienne emitted a friendly, charming, warm vibe. He truly liked most of humanity and enjoyed their company. But he turned on the menacing vibes in a huge way when he chose to. And he chose to make Tim as terrified as possible.

He looked Tim directly in the eye, latched onto his freewill and crooked a single finger for Tim to come forward. He could smell Tim's terror, his victims always wanted to refuse and remain on the safe side of the cell. Disobedience didn't have a chance in hell of happening. Like a wooden soldier, he walked stiff–legged, one forced step at a time.

Tim's legs stopped their forward motion mere inches from him. Etienne's hand shot out and grabbed his victim's jaw in a steel grip just short of crushing the bone, forcing him to look directly into his eyes. "You will move to Las Vegas and never return to

V.A. Dold

Louisiana. You have no desire to ever see Anna again. If you ever try to see her without her invitation, you will become violently ill. That illness will not be relieved until all thoughts of seeing Anna without permission fade from your brain. You will cease all association with the syndicate of New Orleans. You will never set foot into a casino or any other form of gambling establishment ever again. You will not say a bad word about Anna to anyone, ever. She is perfect in all ways and your failed marriage is completely your fault. You will never endeavor to take advantage of your children in anyway. These orders will remain with you until you take your last breath. If you defy these orders by contacting Anna or attempting to see her in person, you will be instantly covered in painful, debilitating boils. If you continue to defy my orders your manhood and scrotum will shrivel and fall off."

Etienne felt his fangs emerge slowly; he tilted his head just right so the light from the bulb made them glisten. He made sure Tim saw the entire show. Pulling his lips back, he hissed into Tim's face causing the little coward to soil himself. Before Tim became too disgusting, he sank his fangs deep, drinking his fill. He didn't try to dull Tim's memories–he wanted him to remember and feel everything. When he was satisfied, he roughly pushed Tim away from him and exited the room. He left him to lay cowering on the floor in his own stench.

Tim would never see Etienne again nor remember exactly where the mansion was located. The vampire who had collected him came into the cell and slapped a rag filled with chloroform over his face again.

215

Cade: Le Beau Brothers

*****

Groggy and blurry eyed, Tim found himself in the middle of his living room floor with soiled jeans, not knowing how he got there. He showered and then dialed the airlines. He needed to fly to Vegas as soon as possible. He was frantic, nothing else mattered but getting on a plane today.

As soon as he landed he went to the nearest cheap hotel for the night. The next morning the greasy man behind the glass window in the lobby directed him to a nearby fleabag apartment. It had taken all of one day to locate the filthy dump he would spend the next year living in.

Little did he know, Etienne had family in positions of power in Las Vegas. He was watched twenty-four - seven very closely by a dozen vampires. Every move he made was monitored, and there was no way he would ever get to Anna ever again.

Chapter 17

Wedding Bells

It had only taken Anna and Cade six weeks to fall into a comfortable routine at home. He worked much of the time from his home office, only going to town for essential meetings.

She quickly learned that her stereotype for a billionaire was completely off base. She knew Cade had money when she first met him. She had no idea how much. His preference for jeans, T–shirts, and biker boots over a suit hid a billionaire several times over. He would wear a suit if needed, but he didn't have to like it. They were too restrictive and didn't fit his personality. He considered them an evil that must be observed when necessary.

She weaned off all of her previous clients and was now the main marketing consultant for the Le Beau family's vast holdings. She spent hours each day pouring over what was being utilized properly and what needed changing. They made a great team.

As they finished breakfast, Cade's phone chimed with a text. It was an update on Tim. He had been followed to the emergency room covered in boils.

Cade: Le Beau Brothers

Etienne had immediately informed him when Tim had gone to Vegas. But, Anna had no clue what had actually been done to her ex–husband, only that the modification had already been handled.

He had heard on three different occasions over the last weeks Tim had become violently ill for no apparent reason. His sources were keeping a close eye on the weasel. It seemed he was still attempting to defy his orders. The stupid little man had better not cross the wrong line or parts would start falling off.

This new information gave him the green light to tell Anna, Tim was gone and wouldn't be back. Not that he doubted Etienne's abilities, he was just being cautious. The second level of punishment had held when Tim had purchased an airline ticket to fly back to New Orleans.

Nervously playing with his coffee cup, he cleared his throat. "Cher, I have news on Tim," he began.

Her head shot up from the newspaper she was reading.

"Etienne forced him to move to Las Vegas and never return." He heard her suck in a breath.

"He's really gone for good?"

"Yes, for good." He took her hand and gave it a soft kiss.

"I never thought I would see the day," she whispered.

Cade had plans for tonight, a special dinner was on the menu. Weeks ago he had given her a ring as a promise to always love her, now he wanted to make it official to the entire world. He needed to make a few calls to set up the arrangements.

She was coming out of her state of shock. "I'm so grateful every day for you. You know that, right?"

"I feel the same way about you. Are you okay, cher? I know this must feel very sudden."

She laughed. "I'm great. I didn't realize I was still carrying such a weight and now it's gone. I feel like dancing."

Grinning at her happiness, he suggested they enjoy a long run chasing and playing until they couldn't run another step.

*****

As he toweled off from his shower he found Anna in the kitchen. After the exciting news, he couldn't possibly work. "Hey, babe, let's spend the day being tourists and play hooky."

She thought about that all of three seconds. "I'd love to."

They had a fabulous day people watching at Jackson Square, having lunch with Richie and generally walking around the Quarter.

As the dinner hour was closing in, he texted Stefan to help with his plans. Within two hours they had reservations for dinner at the Red Grill in a private room few knew of.

"How about dinner in town tonight? I don't feel like cooking, do you?"

"I'd love to eat before we go home. Where would you like to have dinner?" she asked. "Anywhere is fine with me."

Cade: Le Beau Brothers

"I have an idea. Just come with me and let me surprise you." He loved making her happy. This was going to be a night to remember.

His brothers had done a bang–up job. The room had soft lighting and candles were on the table covered in a beautiful linen tablecloth. They had even managed to get a mini–grand piano brought in and a young man played quietly for them.

She smiled at him with her heart in her eyes. "You're always doing such sweet things for me. How'd you plan all of this without my knowing?"

"Some days having half a dozen brothers comes in handy. I sent a few texts and like magic we have this romantic dinner." He grinned.

After ordering champagne and hors d'oeuvres, he took her hand in his, playing with his ring on her finger. Slowly, without losing eye contact, he went down on one knee at her feet. "Anna, my love, would you honor me by being my wife as well as my mate?"

Her hand went to her mouth as she gasped in surprise. With happy tears swimming in her eyes she said, "Yes. Oh, yes, I'd love to be your wife."

He gathered her in his arms kissing her deeply. "I love you so much. You have just made me the happiest man in the world."

He kissed her deeply again pouring everything he was into it and taking everything she was in return.

As they ate dinner, they discussed wedding options. They both agreed a church wedding wasn't what they wanted. A quiet civil ceremony at his parents' home was the perfect choice.

*****

After breakfast the next morning Cade called and made all the arrangements. All that was left was to call her boys.

Anna walked into his office. "Cade, would you make a Skype call with me to Thomas and John? I would like to introduce you to them."

"Absolutely. I would love to meet your sons."

She set her laptop on the coffee table in front of them.

Luckily, they were both home, and in minutes everyone was in what amounted to the same virtual room. "Thomas, John, I would like to introduce you to my fiancé, Cade. Cade, this is Thomas and John."

"Hello, Cade. I've heard a lot about you. It's nice to finally meet you." John was always the accepting one.

"Fiancé, Mom? Really? Isn't this a little fast?" Thomas was her protector as usual.

"No, Thomas, it isn't. I'd love to have you come for our ceremony here at the plantation."

"That's great, Mom. When?" John was always one hundred percent Anna's son, her personal cheering section. He was all for her new relationship.

"Two weeks from now on Saturday. If you are willing to come, we will send you airline tickets and pick you up at the airport. I'd love it if you stayed for a few days, but if you have a case which requires you back home on Monday, I understand."

"Mom, I'd like to speak privately with Cade for a minute. Do you mind if we have a little time alone?" Thomas wore a very serious, all business expression.

Cade: Le Beau Brothers

"Go ahead, cher. I'd like to have a chat with him. How about you call John back in the bedroom and I'll let you know when we're done." He knew Thomas needed to make sure his mother was never hurt again. These two young men adored their mother and despised their father. He had always been hurtful and abusive to her in front of them, and they were very protective of her because of that history.

"Okay, Thomas. What would you like to talk about?" He knew he had to meet Thomas as a man and not her son.

"You do know I'm a trained cop, right? That I carry a gun? A loaded gun?"

He had to work very hard to not smile at Thomas's zealous need to protect the woman he loved. He didn't understand she was more loved and protected than any human woman would ever be.

"Yes, I do know that. Your mother is very proud of you. I know you watched your mother suffer for many years with your father. I also know you would kill any man who dared to ever treat her like that again, and that promise is not an idle threat from a man like you." Cade let Thomas know he understood where he was coming from and how seriously he took this.

"I can guarantee, Thomas, I'll never treat her with anything other than complete respect. Your mother is my very heart and soul. If she died, I would literally follow her to the grave. I would never live a day in this world without her. I love her more than anything and I would give my very life to protect her and have the privilege to love her."

Thomas scrutinized him a minute longer and then nodded his head once. "I believe you. I give you my permission to marry my mother. I've done a lot of research on you and, needless to say, had you followed and watched for the past few weeks. You are what you say you are. A fantastic businessman, but also a man who puts family first. I want that for my mother, she deserves better than what she had with my father."

"Thank you, Thomas, your blessing means a lot to me. I'm going to call your mother back in, if that's okay."

"Yes, please, have her come back."

He settled her back on the couch and got John back on Skype. "Okay, boys, should I order tickets for you?" he asked.

She looked so hopeful, neither of the boys could deny her. This was perfect, her family would be there for her on the big day.

*****

Two weeks sped by. Today he was going to marry the woman of his dreams, literally. His tailor had dropped everything to make him a new suit. He thought he looked good, but Anna's opinion would be the one important to him.

Thomas and John flew in the night before and were hanging with him and his brothers. He enjoyed spending time with his soon–to–be stepsons, both young men had very good heads on their shoulders. He hoped for Anna's sake they would decide to relocate to the New Orleans area, she really missed having them near her.

Simon wasn't able to hold human form for more than a few minutes, because of that, he lay resting in his room. The younger three brothers weren't able to make it home on such short notice. Locating them in the South American jungle had proven difficult.

He and the rest of the men had been confined to the main house. They were not allowed to step foot outside the door no matter what, per his mother's instructions.

"I could really use a drink. Who would like to join me?" Cade asked.

There was of chorus of 'I would' from the men around the great room. Stefan volunteered to make the drinks while Marcus searched for something they could snack on. The waiting was beginning to wear on everyone and drinks with a little food would be a nice distraction.

Marcus was asking if anyone would like a refill when his mother walked in with the Justice of the Peace Judge Tibadou. Cade introduced him to the men before they took their places on the front lawn to await his Anna.

His father walked his mother to the archway that Anna would enter through, before joining him to stand as his best man. He glanced at the leader of the small orchestra hired to play for the ceremony and received a thumbs up, they were ready and waiting for his signal to begin.

His mother gave him a wave and with a nod to the band, the music Anna had chosen filled the air. His mother was beautiful as she came towards him, her face was shining with joy for him. She took her place with them as Matron of Honor. He held his breath, any moment and he would see her come into view.

The music changed tempo as Thomas and John

stepped through the arbor with his mate. She was flanked on both sides by her handsome sons. He couldn't breathe, she was stunning.

How did I manage to be gifted with such a beauty? he wondered.

His father gave him a little nudge to bring him back to his senses as Anna and her boys stopped in front of him. Thomas was very serious in his role as the eldest son, as he made a show of presenting his mother's hand to Cade. Her sons had accepted him as her choice and this was his way of showing he was onboard.

Cade reverently brought her to stand next to him as the judge led them through the traditional vows and the answered I do's. The formal service was brief, only lasting five minutes, ending with them being presented as man and wife. The phrase was music to his ears. Wrapping her in his arms, he thoroughly kissed his new wife.

Many in the local shifter community had come to the wedding, filling every available chair. Finding a mate was often difficult, and as such, was celebrated by everyone. Add to that, the pack considered them the royal family and their future king was taking his queen.

He tucked his arm behind her knees and picked her up, carrying her down the aisle to the reception area with Anna giggling all the way.

Isaac was the star for the rest of the day, creating delicious treats and directing activities like a maestro. He was famous in the area for his barbeques and they were more than happy to let him take over the reception.

Cade: Le Beau Brothers

As the first round of steaks hit the grill's surface they cut the cake. Anna enjoyed feeding Cade his piece, wiping a smear of frosting off his chin with heat in her gaze. He audibly groaned, this may end up being a very long afternoon if she kept looking at him like that.

Shifter weddings can go well into the night and often end in a pack run when the bride and groom retire.

*****

A couple of hours later, Anna was showing signs of fatigue; time to go home and have a private celebration.

They thanked everyone for coming. Then they took a few minutes to speak with Richie, and said their goodnights. It was official. They were now married in every way.

The moment the bride and groom retired for the night and the two humans went to bed, the band adjusted their play list and switched from wedding dance music to cover band songs. Bad moon rising, Blue moon, Shame on the Moon, and even Li'l Red Riding Hood. After a half dozen songs and a lot of whooping and howling, the entire reception prepared to shift. As Anna's best friend, Richie had been given the honor of leading the pack run to celebrate their new princess, an honor he was proud of and took seriously.

Standing on the band's stage, he waited for the last song to end and the crowd to quiet before he began. "We have been blessed by our Goddess with our future queen, an incredible woman that I am proud to call my friend. Let us raise our glasses in a toast to our future king and queen."

The band set their instruments aside and raised their glasses with the crowd. As one, everyone shouted the traditional shifter toast, "To Prince Cade and Princess Anna. May they live a long and happy life together."

Every empty glass was then thumped on the tabletops three times, another long–held tradition.

Once the crowd quieted again, Richie placed the microphone in its stand and held up his right arm. The instant he dropped it to his side, every wolf in the place shifted. It was a spectacular sight to behold. Wolves of every color stood before Richie waiting.

A moment later, a rich solid black wolf with shining brown eyes swished it's tail and leapt from the stage. An eerie chorus of yips and howls was heard as it faded into the forest and the pack disappeared from sight.

*****

The next morning Cade sat quietly with his first cup of coffee. Anna was still asleep, so he had a small window of opportunity to make plans without her knowing. He wanted to give his new bride a wedding gift from his heart, not from his wallet. She had asked her best friend, Rose, to come, but she hadn't been able to get the time off at such short notice. He knew not having Rose at the wedding had hurt her. So, he decided to make it up by arranging a surprise visit from Rose at Thanksgiving.

Cade: Le Beau Brothers

The boys had spent the night at the main house to give the newly married couple privacy. He had to search a bit to locate them but eventually found them nursing hangovers by the river.

He pulled them aside and arranged a visit from them as well, and then called Rose to coordinate with her. Within an hour, he had the surprise set and could hardly wait for Thanksgiving to give her this gift.

Chapter 18

Several months later

Cade let Isaac and Emma in on the secret visit of Rose, John and Thomas. Isaac was in charge of collecting the young men from the airport and hiding them at the main house until he gave the signal. They were keeping him informed on the flight by text. From the last message he received, the plane had landed and they were claiming their luggage. He expected his parents to arrive with the boys in about forty five minutes.

They were settled in front of the television watching a zombie series Anna loved. The episode would end right after he expected the car to pull in at his parents, perfect timing. When the show ended he would get her to go outside with him and then signal the boys to come over.

"Close your eyes," he breathed, cupping her face gently in his large warm hands, blocking her view. He kissed her cheeks, trailing kisses to her cute little nose, then feather light, over her lids. Her breath was warm on his face as he leaned his forehead against hers. As at the wedding, before the boys got close enough to see her younger looks from the conversion, he used his magic to make her appear the mid–forties woman like they would expect. They heard footsteps as the boys came near, leaves crunching and twigs snapping. He had them stop about five feet away.

Cade gave her one last kiss as he released her face and he took one step back from her. "All right, you can open your eyes now."

When she opened them, her hand flew to her mouth as she gasped. The reality of what she was seeing hit her then, and a squeal of happiness erupted from her as she launched herself at the two humans she loved most in the world. She was not a weepy woman, but she'd missed them terribly and her eyes misted and threatened to expose her girly side. She latched onto first one, then the other. "Oh, my God! I can't believe you are here! How long can you stay? Are you having Thanksgiving with us? When did you get here? Oh, my God!!!! You are really here!!" When she finally let go, she asked Cade with delight glistening in her eyes, "How'd you know I missed them so badly?" Everyone laughed at her excited, nonstop stream of questions. She shot them out so fast she almost sounded like an auctioneer. No one had a chance to answer one question before she asked the next.

"I'm like Merlyn, I know things," He teased. *Remember, I not only hear your thoughts when you allow me to, but I feel what you feel. You missed them and it was important to you that you spend Thanksgiving together. It mattered to you so it mattered to me.*

Anna had the biggest smile he had ever seen on her face. She was as close to glowing as a person could get. She tucked one arm in the crook of each of the boys' arms and marched them into the house.

"Where's your luggage?" She realized they weren't carrying any with them.

"We left the bags at Isaac's house." Thomas gestured over his shoulder with his thumb. "Cade was hiding us until he had you in position for the surprise. We'll go and get them in a bit. So how are you, Mom?"

"I'm great. And even better now you both are here. I still can't believe you surprised me!"

John was discretely trying to look around, but she saw him craning his neck down the hall.

"Would you like a tour, John? She hadn't had the opportunity to show off the house when they came for the wedding. The boys had flown in and out in less than twenty–four hours. The house had been overflowing with tables and chairs for the reception. Of course, there was the whole 'no kids sharing my wedding night' aspect, too. She had her hands on her hips and still wore an ecstatic smile.

"Sure, that would be great." She almost laughed as he tried to sound uninterested. John was always the curious one.

She loved the flowing and yet sectioned–off home Cade had built. On a day–to–day basis, the family lived in one half of the house, and when company visited there was a complete wing just for them.

As you came in through the front door, off to the right was a small, formal sitting room, and then you stepped into the great room. From here you could go left into the master suite or right into the formal dining room, kitchen, laundry room, extra bathroom, and a bedroom, which would one day be a nursery.

As she stood and waited for the men to join her, she gestured toward the master suite. "Right through there is our master bedroom. No need for you boys to go in there." The boys rolled their eyes at their mother. She led the group into the center area of the house, which she considered the heart of the home.

"As you can see, we have a full chef's kitchen with informal seating. To the left is a formal dining room. To the right down the hall are the laundry room and a spare bedroom. Feel free to make yourself at home, grab some food or a drink, anything you need." They passed through the kitchen and into an area that marked the start of the separate wing located behind the garage and beyond.

"Cade, you have a great place here," John said.

"Yeah. Man, did you have this built custom?" Thomas asked.

"Actually I did design the entire layout and then had an architect draw up plans."

Anna got the group moving again, and they stepped into a large, long room running the length of the three–car garage. Thomas and John looked at each other and grinned. They stood in a recreation room complete with wet bar and pool table. There was even a sitting area with leather couches and La–Z–Boy chairs facing a 60–inch flat screen hung over a wood burning fireplace. Oh, yeah, they were going to have some fun. You had to pass through the recreation room to get to the actual guest wing of the house. Behind Anna's back, the boys high–fived each other and Cade chuckled.

She put her hands on her hips, looked at her sons and said, "We have three bedrooms back here. One of them is a complete guest suite with its own living room. You two can figure out who gets which room on your own. Leave me out of the battle." She saw the gleam in their eyes as they tried to figure out how they could finagle the private guest suite.

She stepped through the door and gestured to the left and to the right. "There are two identical bedrooms with a walkthrough bathroom shared in between. Beyond that is the guest suite with full bath, bedroom and living room. Figure out which room you're taking and then you should probably go back to Isaac's and get your luggage before it gets too late. Now, come here and give your mom another hug. I still can't believe you're both here." She gave them both quick hugs and then left them to figure out their rooms.

Back in the great room, she wrapped her arms around Cade's waist and smiled up at him. "Have I told you lately what a wonderful man you are?"

"I'm not sure you have. Perhaps you can tell me and then show me." He had a mischievous, crooked smile and a sparkle in his eyes.

She slid her arms up around his neck and pulled his lips down to hers in a passionate kiss. She could never kiss him only once. They were still wrapped in a tight embrace when Thomas and John came out of the guest wing to head out of the house.

"That is so wrong. Get a room!" Thomas yelled as they went out the door.

John just blushed and looked away.

Cade: Le Beau Brothers

In no time, they returned loaded down with luggage and went to the guest wing to unpack. Since it was already late, they said a quick goodnight to their mother and Cade and headed off to bed.

*****

Anna decided to treat the boys to a full breakfast the next morning. She woke Cade and the boys with the delicious smells of freshly brewed coffee and bacon frying. She grinned to herself, it worked every time.

He wrapped his arms around her, nuzzled her neck and kissed her bare shoulder.

Bonjour, ma belle mate, mon amour.

She leaned back and laid her head against Cade's shoulder smiling to herself while she continued flipping the bacon.

Good morning yourself, my sexy wolf.

Cade's chest rumbled against her back, a sure sign both man and beast were content.

*****

She had just finished chopping fresh vegetables, grating the cheese, and she was cracking eggs for the veggie omelets when both of the boys came stumbling out of the guest wing. John was brushing his sleep–rumpled hair out of his eyes and Thomas was scratching the back of his neck.

"Smells so good," John said through a yawn.

Thomas just growled, "Coffee."

"I take it that means you would like a cup of coffee, Thomas?" Anna said in irritation at his rude demand.

Thomas decided it may be safest to rephrase himself. "Mom, the coffee smells great. May I have a cup?"

"Why, yes. I can get that for you," she said with humor in her voice and a smile. Thomas was always grumpy in the morning.

While the men enjoyed their coffee, she quickly made up four omelets and they sat down to breakfast.

"Man, that was great, Mom. I miss your cooking," John said.

"Yeah, we can't find women back home who can cook like you, Mom." Thomas added.

"You boys can both move on down here. We'll help you find good women," Cade volunteered.

Anna's face lit up at the thought of even the slightest possibility her sons would move closer. She knew her boys, and if she brought up the subject of them moving to Louisiana, the first thing they would do is put on the brakes. With them, she had to make them think moving was their idea. The wheels in her mind were already turning.

"Do you two have plans for the day?" Anna asked.

"Since we are so close to New Orleans and the French Quarter, we thought we would go into town for the day," Thomas said.

"I think my brother, Stefan, is heading into town in about an hour if you'd like to catch a ride with him. I know he plans to be there all day."

"Then we'd better get cleaned up. Does he live close by?" John asked.

"Actually most of us have houses scattered around the plantation. Stefan's house is about ten acres to the west. I'll give him a call and make sure he stops by and picks you up."

About an hour later everyone was dressed, buffed and polished, ready for the day. Those boys sure did clean up well. Look out New Orleans girls, you are about to get your hearts broken by the boys from Denver.

Stefan knocked once and then let himself in through the front door. "Hello in the house," which was Stefan's normal greeting when he came to visit.

Cade made the introductions. "Stefan, you remember Thomas and John, Anna's sons from Denver." The men each stepped forward in turn and shook hands, greeted each other the way men do with slapping backs and bumping fists. With no further fanfare, they headed out the door to enjoy the day.

Cade had work to do in his home office and Anna decided to start preparing for Thanksgiving. Everyone would be busy until at least dinnertime.

Tomorrow was Thanksgiving, and that meant she had a lot to do.

*****

Thomas and John returned a little earlier than she had planned. She was still busy in the kitchen and really needed them occupied and out from underfoot.

Babe, would you show the boys around and keep them busy for an hour or so until I'm finished?

Anything you need, mon amour.

"Why don't I show you boys around the plantation while your mom finishes up?" he asked as he gave her a little conspiratorial wink.

"That would be great. Do you have any fishing gear, Cade? Maybe tomorrow we could wet a line." Thomas loved to fish and sadly got little opportunity to enjoy it back home.

"I have a variety of fresh water and salt water gear. Whatever is your pleasure." Cade's excitement over Thomas's shared love of fishing had him looking like a little boy. He hadn't had a fishing buddy since Simon joined the Marines.

"Great, we'll get changed into jeans for the tour and take a look at the gear," Thomas said.

Once the men returned from their tour, dinner was served. The boys were in heaven–pot roast with mashed potatoes and gravy. They basically ate in silence except for the occasional moan of appreciation coming from Thomas and John.

"I know I taught you two how to cook when I was raising you. What is with the 'I haven't eaten a good meal in forever' act?" she asked.

"Oh, we know how to cook, we just don't," John said.

"I told you, cher, restaurants are essential to the survival of a single man."

"Exactly," both boys said together.

They all laughed and helped clear the table.

The evening went by too fast for Anna's liking. She cherished every minute with her boys. Dinner was eaten, and the kitchen cleaned. She could finally relax with her family.

Chapter 19

MOM is a WOLF!!!

Thomas and John were exhausted and had gone to bed. This was the perfect time for a quick run to relax after cooking all day.

The property was beautiful with tall, old–growth trees with lovely Spanish moss hanging from the branches, some hanging to the ground. In some areas of the property, the trees were so thick even a wolf barely got through. In other areas, they were spread out like a sprawling lawn with a tree here and a tree there.

Anna's favorite time to run the property was when there was a heavy, gray fog. The murkiness gave everything an air of mystery and made playing hide and seek much more fun.

You had to be careful running the woods even as a wolf. In the New Orleans area, the trees tend to have a heavy root system running above the ground, and you can easily catch a paw or trip. She knew this from experience, spraining a paw was something she didn't care to endure again.

The Le Beau plantation, held by Isaac, was set to be handed down from generation to generation. It was lush with a variety of areas to enjoy. There was the riverfront with aged trees hanging their branches until they dipped into the water with its cool breezes. There was also the heavily wooded area and the bayou with its gators, nutria and all the multitudes of birds and wildlife the habitat supports.

The original plantation house which Isaac and Emma lived in was closer to the river portion of the property to take advantage of the cooling effects for the house in the heat of summer.

Barely out of the house and still on the porch, Cade shifted, swished his tail at her, then bounded into the night. She was still new to the whole shifting thing, and the effort took a little more concentration and a lot more time for her to get it right.

Dang it! I'm going to get good at this if it kills me.

This time the change took her a minute or so, but she was actually able to accomplish the process correctly!

Score!!!

She was in the process of congratulating herself and Cade was jumping circles around her in his wolf form when they heard a strangled noise coming from the screen door. Thomas and John had come out of their rooms where she thought they were sleeping and watched their mother change into a wolf in front of their eyes.

He sighed and nudged her wolf in the side with his muzzle.

Come on, cher, no run tonight. We have other matters to handle now.

Cade: Le Beau Brothers

He walked to the bottom of the stairs leading to the porch and pointedly stared the young men in the eye, then shifted back to human form. His change at their feet had them stumbling back a step, gasping. "Come on, boys, let's give your mother a little privacy to shift back. She's still learning and the process requires a little effort."

The men settled into the great room and waited for her to join them. No one said a word. They stared at Cade like he was an alien. John kept craning his neck to view Cade from different angles like he might spot some fur sprouting.

Anna, anytime.

Sorry, but the shock and pressure is giving me a little trouble. I almost got it.

Moments later, she walked through the door and stood in front of her sons with her hands on her hips like only a mother can do.

She looked each of them directly in the eye. "Come on, let's hear it. Hit me with your questions." She waved her hand toward herself indicating, bring it on.

She saw Cade suppressing a grin as he watched her dealing with her adult boys.

You are poetry in motion and, damn, I'm never going to get myself into a situation where you look at me like that.

She turned and gave him a glare.

"What the hell was that?!" John pointed in the direction of the porch.

"Damn, Mom, are you a freaking werewolf!!?" Thomas exclaimed.

She glared at them and then the 'mom pointed

finger' came into action. "Watch your language and DO NOT take that tone with me."

The familiar interaction from their mother worked some kind of magic on the boys. They calmed a bit and began what would be a long information–gathering session.

John and Thomas glanced at each other. "Are we shifters and you never told us?" Thomas asked.

"No, you are one hundred percent normal human. Before you freak out, let me explain what you saw." She sat next to Cade and took a breath preparing herself for the best plan of action and explanation.

"I'm not a werewolf, I'm a shifter, which is different. From what I understand, werewolves as you see in movies and read about in books come from tales told by people who accidentally see a shifter who has gone rogue."

She held up her hand like a stop sign as they geared up to shoot questions at her.

"Let me say up front there was no violent attack involved to make a shifter like in the werewolf movies." She wanted to reassure her sons shifters were not a bad thing.

For the next two hours, Anna and Cade answered the scores of questions from the boys.

"You mentioned a rogue shifter. What causes them to go bad?" Thomas asked.

"Having a combined soul is the main reason a shifter would go rogue. If his or her mate is killed, they also lose half of their soul, which has been fused together by magic. The rending of a soul is horrible and often impossible to withstand for the mate left behind. Usually the other mate will die as well. On occasion a shifter will go a bit nuts and let his wolf take over in a rage. This normally occurs due to the death of their mate when they fail to follow them in death. They can't be brought back from the edge and saved. They're killed to protect the shifters' secrecy and humans from harm."

Thomas looked at Cade speculatively, "So that's what you meant when you said you would literally follow her to the grave."

Cade silently nodded.

"So, Mom, can we be shifters, too?" John's eyes sparkled with interest.

"There are two ways to become a shifter. The main way is to mate with your other half who was born a shifter. The other way, which is extremely rare, is to petition the Goddess for conversion. She is the one who originally created the shifters, and on rare occasions she'll bless a human with shifting abilities and make them one. If you were to decide to try to be a shifter, Emma would request that of the great Luna."

"Let me get this straight. Cade turned you into a shifter." Thomas gave Cade a glare.

"Yes, he did. But only after I said I wanted him to, so put that attitude away."

John was still bursting with questions. "Are shifters like immortal kind of things? I mean, do you only live to be normal human age, or what?"

Cade joined in again. "Shifters live to be around fourteen hundred years old. At maturity, a shifter appears to be around twenty–five to thirty years old and they remain that way until they are about nine hundred years old, and then they begin to very slowly age again. So in reality, your mother looks like she is in her twenties. I'm using magic to make her appear as you would expect her to."

"So what do you really look like, Mom?" John asked.

Cade cocked an eyebrow and she was in her twenties right before their eyes.

"WHOA!" they both exclaimed.

She let out a giggle. "I know, right?"

Thomas leaned forward. "Geez, Mom, you look hot."

"Ewwww." John punched him in the arm.

"Not like that, you idiot. I just mean she is a very attractive woman."

Cade smiled. "I couldn't agree more." His eyes started to glow as he allowed steamy thoughts to race through his mind.

"As long as I have you all grossed out, John, I might as well tell you in my case the conversion to shifter made me physically younger and I can have children again."

"Oh, man, Mom. TMI." John blushed and covered his face with his hands, shaking his head back and forth like he might be able to dispel the unwelcome knowledge.

"All right, boys, enough questions for tonight. Write down anything you think of and we can answer you tomorrow." She was already standing and yawning, ready for the night to end.

Cade: Le Beau Brothers

Epilogue

Thanksgiving

The family gathered at Cade and Anna's house.
As Anna scanned the room, she noted what everyone
was wearing. Once dinner was prepared she would
need to change her clothes. Thomas and John were in
blue jeans and short–sleeved shirts. They were used to
Denver winters, and to them this was absolutely
balmy. Stefan was dressed in blue jeans, a button down
white shirt and a leather jacket. Cade also wore blue
jeans, but he had on a black button–down dress shirt
and loafers. As always, Marcus was dressed a little bit
more formal than the rest of them, he did like his
fashion. Marcus came in dress pants and a crisp, white
designer shirt. Simon was curled up on the couch in his
wolf form. With Anna's help he now only spent about
half his time as a wolf.

"You're all looking so handsome today," Anna
said entering the room. She knew any reference to
Cade's brothers being handsome would push his
buttons. He was just too easy and she couldn't help
herself.

"Cher, you don't need to be noticing other men," he growled.

She laughed as she walked toward the kitchen. Marcus and Stefan turned to each other, looked at him, and both busted out laughing.

Anna quickly got busy in the kitchen making a list of what still needed to be done and when items needed to start cooking so everything finished at the same time. There was still so much to do before her final guests arrived.

Every time Cade tried to sneak into the kitchen, she would shoo him back out. The aromas wafting through the house were making the men salivate.

Stefan glanced at Cade. "I know she cooks for you at home all the time, but did you know she could cook like this? I mean, man that smells good. You need to find me a woman who can cook like that."

He grinned. "No, I didn't, but I'm an even luckier wolf now. Every time I turn around my mate amazes me more. Sorry, brother, you're on your own. I don't know how I ever got so lucky as to stumble upon Anna, but I thank the Goddess every day I did."

Marcus nodded in agreement. "Yeah, I agree. Being a bachelor's getting really old. I'm looking forward to settling down with a beautiful woman and starting a family."

He glanced between both of his brothers. "Anna has spoken of several girlfriends who are single, and you are going to get to meet Rose today. Who knows…" He left it hang there for his brothers to think about.

Rose, was flying in from Denver to celebrate Thanksgiving as a surprise. She would be staying for an open–ended visit. When Cade heard she had lost her job, he had called and suggested she extend her stay with them.

When Anna had her back turned, Stefan snuck into the kitchen driven in by the wonderful smells wafting around him. He was about to stick his finger into the mashed potatoes when Anna struck.

"Get out of that!" she snapped, cracking his knuckles with a spoon.

"Ow!" he yelped, shaking his fingers before sticking them in his mouth to suck away the pain.

"Get out of here, Stefan, or I swear I'll whack you again."

"Fine, I'll wait little sister, but you're killing me here." He grabbed a couple of beers from the cooler and went back to the men.

When he entered the great room, Cade took one look at his bright red hand and a huge grin lit across his face. "What did you do little brother?"

Stefan scowled at him. "Your mate wields one nasty wooden spoon. I made the mistake of reaching for the mashed potatoes. They just smelled so good! I only wanted a little taste, and bam! She whacked me with her evil spoon." Stefan was gesturing wildly mimicking a replay of what happened in the kitchen.

John and Thomas sat with knowing smiles.

"Oh, yeah, that sounds like Mom all right," Thomas said.

Both Cade and Marcus busted out laughing; even Simon made a chuffing sound from the couch.

A car was heard as it pulled into the driveway. Cade reached over and gently touched Simon's shoulder. "Simon, I'm sorry, but could you please shift to human? Anna's human friend is about to walk through the door."

Everyone turned to the sound of the front door opening. Isaac, Emma, and Rose walked in carrying suitcases. Hearing the commotion, Anna came hustling out of the kitchen wiping her hands. She couldn't believe what she was seeing! Both women squealed, grabbed each other and started a hugging dance combination. Everyone smiled and waited for the women to finish their excited greeting of each other.

She let Rose go from the tight hug she had her in, wrapped her arm around her friend's shoulder, and they both turned to face the room full of handsome men and her mother–in–law. "Rose, you know John and Thomas, and you've already met Isaac and Emma. This extremely handsome piece of male specimen is my husband, Cade."

He stepped forward, taking Rose's hand in both of his. Clasping them gently, he said, "Rose, it's a sincere pleasure to meet you. I'm so glad you're able to spend some extended time with us."

"I'm glad I was able to come. I hated to miss the wedding. I'm sure the service was beautiful."

"I wish you could've been here as well, but we can make up for it now." Anna gave her friend another squeeze. "This scoundrel is the second oldest of the family, Stefan. Stefan, this is Rose. The one with impeccable manners is Marcus. Marcus, please meet Rose."

Each of them stepped forward and gallantly shook Rose's hand as they strangely leaned in, and she swore they sniffed her.

Cade: Le Beau Brothers

Anna gestured to Simon lying with his eyes closed on the couch. "You remember I told you about Simon. He's not feeling well, but wanted to join us today. He'll come to the table for dinner if he's feeling up to it, otherwise I'll set a plate aside for him for later."

Rose stared at Simon, lying with his back to everyone in the room. Then she walked to him, reached out and gently touched his shoulder with her fingertips. The caress was really barely a touch at all. She blushed bright red and pulled her hand back, quickly glancing at Simon's family before returning to stand next to Anna again.

Anna saw Simon's head raise a little and turn toward Rose. His nose seemed to twitch, but as Rose retreated he returned to his original position.

"Are you all right?" Anna whispered leading Rose into the kitchen.

"I don't know. I don't just walk up to strangers and touch them like that. Why did I do that?" she asked.

"Don't worry about it, hon. Let's enjoy the meal and we can talk tonight after everyone goes home. I don't think anyone was watching anyway," she said to comfort her. She knew darn well everyone had seen her, but she wasn't going to tell her friend that.

With introductions out of the way, everyone started milling around chatting and enjoying each other's company. Anna encouraged Rose to join the boys, along with Isaac and Emma, in the great room while she went to change out of her cooking clothes into a pair of black slacks and a silk blouse for dinner.

Cade quietly snuck through the bedroom door,

easing it shut behind him. He leaned against the wall, quietly watching her, admiring his beautiful mate. He couldn't stand to be away from her for very long.

Not hearing him, she turned around expecting to be alone. "Oh my God! You scared the heck out of me. Don't do that."

He tried to appear contrite. "I'm sorry, cher. I didn't mean to startle you. I couldn't wait one more second to get you all to myself. I swear I'll never get enough of you."

She gave him a saucy smile, stood on her tiptoes and gave him a sweet, gentle kiss.

When he moved to snag her, she quickly danced out of his reach. "Oh, no, you don't. I need to get cleaned up and changed so we can eat before all my hard work gets cold."

He gave her his best pout, sure he looked like a petulant child.

She chuckled and shook her head as she entered the bathroom and closed the door, locking it for good measure.

A few minutes later she appeared back with the others. She had taken her hair down and left the mass flowing gently down her back.

Cade could hardly breathe she was so beautiful. He stood from where he was sitting and caressed her cheek gently with his fingertips. "You take my breath away."

She smiled and leaned into his palm for a moment. Turning, she addressed the room, "If everyone will move to the dining room, dinner is ready. Emma and Rose, would you please help me bring in the food?"

Cade: Le Beau Brothers

Isaac stood and gave Anna a warm, fatherly hug. "You are lovely, Anna, as always," giving her a knowing wink.

The party moved to the dining room and the Thanksgiving dinner was placed on the table. Six pairs of male eyes almost popped out of their heads.

Cade gazed at Anna. "You did all this? Everything looks and smells amazing."

"I had a little help." She glanced at Emma. "But, yes, the recipes are mine."

She held out the carving knife to Isaac. "Would you like to honor us by carving the turkey?"

With a happy little grin, Isaac inclined his head and accepted the honor.

Once the platters were loaded with sliced turkey, the feast began as the bowls and platters were passed around the table. Everything was perfect. The turkey was juicy and succulent, the mashed potatoes were rich and creamy, and Anna's family recipe for hamburger dressing was the absolute hit of the meal.

Cade watched with pride as everyone piled their plates to overflowing. He leaned in and kissed Anna's cheek gently. "You've done an amazing job, mon amour."

He passed the mashed potatoes across her to Stefan, who gazed at them with a fierce longing. "Do I have to share these?" he asked.

Anna laughed. "Take as much as you want, there's more in the kitchen."

The room quickly filled with moans of delight as the men began eating.

Stefan was on his third helping of potatoes and gravy as the desserts were served.

Anna looked around the table at the men who were quickly becoming her new family. "I made my family's favorites, pumpkin pie and strawberry rhubarb pie. I hope you like them."

Thomas and John both said together, "Oh, yeah, Mom's strawberry rhubarb pie is the absolute best."

From the amount of damage done to the pies when everyone was finished, Anna would take that as a yes.

Everyone sat back in their chairs, full and content. Now was the perfect time for their announcement. "We'd like everyone's attention for a minute." Everyone quieted and waited to hear what Anna had to say. "Why don't you tell them, babe?"

"Mom, Dad, in about six months you'll be grandparents," Cade announced.

The cheering was deafening with everyone congratulating them.

Thomas and John high fived. "Is it a little brother or little sister, Mom?" John asked.

"We don't know yet, hon. I'm not sure if we want to find out ahead of time." Anna was so happy the boys were taking their news so well.

"Rose, do you think you will be able to stay long enough to see my baby into the world?" Anna really wanted her there.

"You couldn't keep me away."

Isaac smiled with his heavy–lidded eyes half closed with satisfaction. He stole a glance in Rose's direction and gave Emma's hand a gentle squeeze under the table.

"Anna that was the most delicious meal. Your talents in the kitchen are second to none," Emma said

251

quietly. "Please let me know if I can be of any help to you with the pregnancy and if you would like a shopping partner for the baby, I offer my services."

Anna could tell Emma was dying to start shopping.

"I can't believe I ate so much. I couldn't stop myself," Cade said as he rubbed his bloated stomach with a satisfied expression on his face.

"Yes, Anna, that was a true work of art," Marcus agreed.

Rose sat quietly watching the family's banter and interaction.

Dinner was cleared away and the party relocated to the great room again. The family was naturally drawn to Simon and his need for touch. Marcus instinctively sat in the chair close to Simon's head, reached out and laid a hand on his brother's shoulder. Simon's sigh at the contact was soft, but all the wolves heard him.

The room was full of activity, loud, boisterous men doing what men do when you get a group of them together.

Stefan spotted Anna across the room with Rose. Walking over to the women, he wiggled his way between them and wrapped one arm around the shoulders of each woman. His wink at her and Rose had Anna shaking her head–he was incorrigible.

Instantly Cade's head jerked up, his eyes latched onto his brother. There was death in those eyes. It was deadly for another male to touch a pregnant mated female. Stefan stiffened when he saw his brother's threatening stare.

V.A. Dold

At the same instant, Simon went from what everyone thought was a sleeping state to full alert. He shot to a sitting position, nose sniffing the air, glaring at his brother with violence evident in his stare. Hidden from Rose's view were Simon's hands which had shifted into the deadly claws of his wolf as it forced its way to the surface.

Marcus instantly grabbed Simon, placing his hands on Simon's shoulders to hold him down on the couch. Isaac had also moved in on the other side of Simon and had his hand on Simons arm to calm him.

Stefan casually removed his arms from around the women, careful to make no sudden moves. Never taking his eyes off Simon, he stepped away from Rose and slowly backed out of the room.

Seeing Stefan move away from Rose allowed Simon the space he needed to control himself and remain seated on the couch. It was taking everything he had to remain in human form and not attack Stefan. Inside his wolf snarled and snapped for release. He knew he had to protect the shifter community and not expose himself to a human. Gritting his teeth, he stayed in control.

"Just breathe, everything's all right, just breathe. Simon, look at your hands. You need to take care of that," Isaac whispered quietly so only Simon would hear.

Simon breathed deeply, closed his eyes and centered himself so he would be able to shift to total human again. That's when he caught the first tendrils of heavenly fragrance coming from Anna's friend. It

253

was the coffee and cinnamon rolls again.

He thought he had smelled it earlier when Rose had touched him, but it had been so fleeting he thought he had imagined it.

All of this happened in a matter of seconds. Rose, hadn't seen most of it, she had missed the violence and fury coming from Simon. She gave Anna a questioning look and then saw the brother called Simon was now sitting up on the couch.

Everyone had shocked expressions on their faces except for Isaac and Emma. They gave each other a wink as Simon stood, straightened his shirt and walked over to Rose. With a spark of life in his eyes no one had seen since he had returned home, he reached for Rose's hand. "It's my pleasure to meet such a beautiful woman."

Simon gave Rose a warm smile. As he took another deep breath, his smile grew a little larger. He held her hand longer than was necessary and gazed deeply into her eyes. "I look forward to spending time with you." He gave a gentle kiss to the back of her hand, inclined his head. Then, walking backward, he led her to the couch with him.

Small gasps of surprise were heard all around the room. It was wonderful to see Simon interact and respond in a way they understood. There had been little hope that the old Simon would return to them. That hope had just increased exponentially.

THE END

V.A. Dold

Please let others know if you enjoyed this title. Please leave a review on the vendor site in which you purchased this title. Reviews help to spread the word and boost overall sales. This means I have more time to write more books in the series you love.

Thank you!

V.A. Dold

Cade: Le Beau Brothers

Read on for an excerpt from

SIMON
Book 2

of the Le Beau Brothers

Prologue: The Plan

Emma Le Beau knelt in front of her altar as she prepared to take her daily meditation time and speak with the spirits when the Goddess came to her. "Simon has suffered much more than any of my children should ever endure. His mate is Rose, a friend to Anna. She will be here at the plantation for Thanksgiving. Her love and connection to Simon will be the final thing he will need to return fully to his human form. I've set events in motion to guarantee Simon's mate will come. Take care, my daughter, blessed be."

The Goddess was the creator of the wolf shifters. Long ago, she blessed a village of humans with wolf souls. They were the first shifters. Since then she has only blessed a handful of humans that were not mated to a born shifter.

Bursting with excitement, Emma ran to Isaac. "I've been given another mate's identity. This woman is meant for Simon."

Isaac's brows furrowed. "Why Simon and not one of the older boys?"

Taking Isaac's hand Emma quietly said, "Fate doesn't work in chronological order. There's nothing type 'A' about fate. Fate does what it wants, when it wants, where it wants, and to whomever it wants. You can't control or dictate fate, it just is.

"The Goddess said our sons would receive their mates at the proper time and then she would disclose to us who that mate was and where she would be found. She never said our sons would receive their mates in order by age from oldest to youngest. We should simply accept the gift she has given and not question her." Emma kissed him, so thankful for her own mate.

"I can see the reasoning behind Simon receiving his mate before Stefan. He's still so withdrawn from his experience. I'm thankful the Goddess wants to ease his suffering by bringing him his destined mate. Especially if she is the answer to completing his healing. It's killing me to see him suffer and not able to help him." Isaac drew Emma in as close as he could get her.

Nibbling on her fingernail Emma said, almost as if speaking to herself, "We need to come up with a plan to get Rose here. The barbecue is tomorrow, and Anna will be here. I'll bring up her friends and family from Denver. If I can get her to mention Rose, I'll point out that Cade's house is very large and has plenty of room for visitors."

"So, plant the seed and let it grow?" Isaac searched her face. "Do you think that will be enough?"

Cade: Le Beau Brothers

"The Goddess said she would come. I'll simply give her the idea for the invitation." Emma's smile was blinding.

"You can be very devious, my love." Isaac nodded in approval. "Okay, it's decided. I will leave the laying of bread crumbs to you."

Isaac happily rubbed his hands together. "This is happening so much faster than I ever dreamed possible. We came up with the idea only a few weeks ago," Isaac said. "When we first planned to help all seven boys find their mates, I was sure it would take years. Our Goddess is moving this along nicely. Once Simon sees Rose and experiences the draw of one mate to another, the unique scent one has for the other, nature will take its course."

Isaac let out a loud belly laugh. "I guess I don't have to worry about the boys going through their long lives without experiencing the incredible love that is enjoyed between mates. Now if we could only get some grandchildren."

Emma sighed wistfully. "I saved many of our baby things from when the boys were born. I would love to hand them down to my grandchildren."

Isaac started to nibble on her neck, and all thoughts of plans flew out the window.

Only a few months ago the first mate disclosed had been Anna, Cade's beautiful mate. Isaac and Emma were thrilled with the results of helping Cade meet his mate. All they had to do was arrange for Cade to meet Isaac for lunch at the Crescent City Brewhouse and then cancel at the last minute.

V.A. Dold

That left Cade free to have a long leisurely lunch with Anna. The love affair and happy ending took off from there. Sure, there was a bump or two in the road, but what great love hasn't had them.

Harassing ex–husbands, dangerous crime bosses, and suspicious adult children have nothing on a Le Beau.

Le Beau Series
Book 1 CADE
Book 2 SIMON
Book 3 STEFAN
Book 4 THOMAS
Book 5 RICHIE (coming soon)
Book 6 LUCAS (coming soon)

And don't miss their follow up HEA's

CADE & ANNA
SIMON & ROSE (coming soon)
STEFAN & EL (coming soon)

CADE

Anna James is single again, finally. In her opinion, men are self-centered and will never love her for who she is, a beautiful, plus-sized woman. All except the fantasy man that she meets in her dreams every night for last five years.

She just never expected her fantasy to be a real live alpha shifter...

Cade Le Beau isn't what he seems. He's a billionaire wolf. A Shifter. He laments his missed chance six months ago to meet his fantasy woman in the flesh. Just as his second chance presents itself, his fantasy woman, his mate, is threatened by the local mob boss and her ex-husband. Now, he has forty-eight hours to deal with this threat once and for all or chance losing her again.

Is it Anna who's in danger, or the humans who unwittingly threaten her?

The heat is on the moment they lay eyes on each other. Neither age, children, horrid ex-husbands nor mob bosses will stop this love affair.

SIMON

Four years of honorably serving his country has left Simon, Cade's younger brother, damaged and trapped in wolf form. Little did he know the only person with the ability to heal him completely would be found at home. Literally. Now that he's found her, he is desperate to claim her.

Rose is a beautiful, voluptuous woman with limited experience with men. Although she's confident, she still has reservations. Never having a family of her own, her fear of abandonment has her fleeing romantic relationships and doubting herself.

Travis is insane. A deadly loose cannon that a secret organization hired to destroy the Le Beau family by denying them their mates. Permanently.

Simon's dream will be lost forever unless he is able to maintain human form.

Cade: Le Beau Brothers

Rose needs unconditional love and a mate to create the family she's always wanted.

Travis's all-consuming drive is to take Rose for himself.

Will Simon ever be whole again, able to claim his mate, giving Rose the love and family she so desperately craves? Or will Travis destroy them both?

STEFAN

El is a beautiful, successful, plus-sized woman suffering a debilitating humiliation that has left her hating all handsome, wealthy men exactly like Stefan Le Beau. Unfortunately for Le Beau, she's known him since she was sixteen and was totally snubbed by him. To her, he's a hound dog and a man-whore.

Stefan is a playboy to the extreme with one hard and fast rule: date a woman only once, take her to bed and be gone before morning. Until El.

Stefan's dream of finding his mate comes true when he bids two hundred thousand dollars to win a date with El at Simon's charity ball. Money well spent in his opinion.

Now, if she would only talk to him. Or look at him. Or touch him, or…like him.

Can Stefan convince El he's a reformed man?

Can El learn to trust a man who is the epitome of what she avoids and could shatter her heart?

It will require drastic, strategic measures from the entire family to make this mating happen.

THOMAS

Julia is happy with her place in the shifter community as the owner of the famous shifter bar, The Backwater. But the life she's created for herself isn't enough to satisfy her crazy-ass mother, Lucinda, who shops her and her sister, Krystal, around to the pure blood shifters like pieces of meat. Only a born shifter mate is good enough for her girls.

Thomas James has his hands full as the shifter king's head of security. He certainly wasn't looking for a girlfriend during the first annual shifter gathering. He had the king and queen to protect, not skirts to chase.

A childhood of emotional and physical abuse by his birth father has left Thomas emotionally unavailable and uninterested in romantic relationships. His father Tim's cruelty to his mother and brother molded him into an extremely protective person. No one messes with his loved ones without answering to him.

Cade: Le Beau Brothers

Even though Julia and Thomas are destined to be mates, the obstacles standing between them and their happily-ever-after seem insurmountable.

Lucinda insists Julia stay away from the filthy human.

Tim is trying to kill every one Thomas loves.

The mysterious Benevolent Sovereign, who is trying to overthrow the throne, has sent swampers to attack Thomas and destroy Julia's livelihood.

With family like theirs, who needs enemies?

Will Julia and Thomas's happiness be snuffed out before it has a chance to begin or will they forge through - obstacles be damned.

CADE & ANNA

When Dr. Marjorie schedules an ultrasound for Anna, Cade begins to go into paranoid meltdown. Something must be wrong! He's sure of it.

Seeing his Daughter on the computer screen larger than life sets Cade onto a path of foolish, well-meaning choices. In a state of panic, he instigates a series of disastrous projects with the Help of Simon, Stefan, and Thomas.

The final disaster lands Cade and Anna stranded on the family's island with Anna in labor and no help in sight.

About the Author

V.A. Dold Amazon best selling author of the Award-winning **Le Beau Series.**

Prior to becoming a full-time writer, she was publicist to the authors, owning ARC Author & Reader Conventions. Still is.

Her idea of absolute heaven is a day in the French Quarter with her computer, her coffee mug, and the Brothers, of course.

A Midwest native with her heart lost to Louisiana; she has a penchant for titillating tales featuring sexy men and strong women. When she's not writing, she's probably taking in a movie, reading, or traveling.

Connect with V.A. Dold:

V.A.'s Website: http://www.vadold.com/

CPSIA information can be obtained at www.ICGtesting.com
Printed in the USA
LVOW12s2247230216

476438LV00001B/13/P

9 780990 523550